SPLIT SCOPE

SPLIT SCOPE

THE SILENCER SERIES BOOK 16

MIKE RYAN

WWW.MIKERYANBOOKS.COM

Copyright © 2021 by Mike Ryan

All rights reserved.

No part of this book may be reproduced in any form or by any electronic or mechanical means, including information storage and retrieval systems, without written permission from the author, except for the use of brief quotations in a book review.

Cover Design by The Cover Collection

1

Recker was sitting at the table, watching Mia walk through the cafeteria doors on her way back to work. Once she disappeared, he pulled out his phone and started looking at it. He usually didn't check it for messages while he was eating with Mia. If it was an emergency, Jones or Haley would call. But he had one text message. It came through about five minutes before that. It was somewhat confusing.

The message was from Michelle Lawson. Recker reread it several times. He couldn't really understand what she was talking about.

"Hey, need to talk to you. Don't leave yet."

By the way she was talking, it almost sounded like Lawson was there. And Recker was sure that couldn't have been the case. Recker's head was down, and didn't see Lawson sitting at another table at the far end of the room. By now, she was just a few feet to his left. She could see the puzzled look on his face.

"I dunno. I thought it was pretty self-explanatory."

Recker knew her voice, so he wasn't alarmed at the sound of someone talking to him that he wasn't expecting. He slowly turned his head and looked up at her, seeing her with a grin on her face.

"Bet you didn't think you'd be seeing me again so soon, huh?"

"Uh, no, I have to say that seeing you here right now is a complete surprise. And I just love surprises."

Lawson laughed. "I know you do. Guess you're wondering why I'm here, huh?"

"Nope. Not at all. Didn't cross my mind in the slightest."

"Yeah, right. Mind if I sit?"

Recker shrugged. "I don't own the table."

Lawson laughed again. "I love your sense of humor. Reminds me of another agent I used to work with. He's retired now, but you two would probably get along great."

"Well maybe when I retire the two of us can go golfing or play backgammon, or whatever it is retired secret agents do."

"Good idea."

Recker held his phone up. "I looked confused because it sounded like you knew where I was and were coming here to talk, and I knew that couldn't be right, because... well, obviously that sounds like you're stalking me or something. And you wouldn't do that, right?"

"What? Me? No!" Lawson threw her hand up and waved it at him for good measure. "Of course I wouldn't do something like that. What do you think I do, work for the CIA or something?"

Recker cleared his throat. "Yeah. Right. So, uh, I guess you're eventually going to tell me why you're here."

"I need your help."

Recker tilted his head and gave her a look. "Michelle."

"Why are you so formal? All my friends call me Shelly. I think we know each other well enough by now."

"Shelly, I really have no interest at the moment in doing some other job for the CIA overseas somewhere. We've got enough going on right here. Chris is still on the mend, and I just don't wanna keep doing that. I'm not on the payroll."

"Good. 'Cause I wasn't asking you."

"You weren't?"

"No. How is Chris, by the way?"

"He's good. Been out of the hospital a few weeks now. He's itching to get back out there, but we've been trying to hold him back as much as possible. Don't think we're gonna be able to keep him back much longer."

"Stubbornness runs in the organization, I see."

Recker grinned. "Apparently. It's a CIA trait, as well. Can't get hired without it. You know the feeling, right?"

"See, another of the things I love about you. You have the great ability to insult people without making it sound like it's an insult."

"You know, if I had known you while I was at the agency, I might still be there."

"Wow, did you just compliment me?"

"Yes, but not on the record. So don't let it go to your head."

"I work for the CIA. You know how it goes, nothing goes to our head. Especially compliments. They're rare enough."

"Now that we've got the pleasantries out of the way, you mind explaining what you're doing here?"

Lawson leaned forward, speaking more softly. "You know, for a former operative, you're getting a little sloppy in your old age."

"My old age?"

"Yeah, see, you and your girlfriend are kind of a known thing nowadays, and you meet her here for lunch quite often. If you were still at the agency, you'd probably get pulled into the office for getting so predictable. You really should change things up every now and then."

Recker smiled, appreciating the humor. "I'll have to start working on that."

"Good idea."

"Now, about what you're actually doing here. With me, specifically."

"Oh. That."

"Yeah. That."

"Well, I wanted to talk to you about working on something."

"See, I knew it. I knew that's what you were here for."

"No, you said for something overseas. It's not overseas."

Recker scrunched his eyebrows together. "You mean it's here?"

"I mean it's here."

"That's all well and good, but I told you before I didn't want to make this a regular thing. And I still don't. I don't work for you guys anymore. And while I'm grateful that I no longer have to worry about anyone from the agency looking for me... I'm done with that life. And I really don't have a desire to go back to it. Even if it's every few months."

"And I get that. I do." She could tell by the look on Recker's face that he didn't quite believe her. "No, I really do. Honest."

"If you did, you wouldn't be here."

A lump went down Lawson's throat. For once, she didn't quite know where to start. Recker could see that she was having more trouble than the last time they met in proposing a deal.

Lawson looked down at the table. "This one's not for the CIA."

"I'm not sure I understand. If it's not for the CIA, then who's it for?"

She lifted her head up and looked Recker in the eyes. "This one's for me."

Recker could see there was some pain behind Lawson's eyes. Whatever this was about, it was personal for her. He sighed, tilted his head down to the side, and put his hand on his forehead before running it over the top of his head. He shouldn't have asked any more questions. He should have just said it wasn't his problem. And he shouldn't have given it any more thought. But since it was Lawson, and he genuinely liked her, he was about to do something he knew he shouldn't. Ask for more details.

"Well, since I'm here, I guess you might as well tell me something about it."

Lawson smiled. "Thanks."

"I haven't agreed to anything yet until I hear the details."

"Of course. This whole thing goes back about a year."

"What whole thing? Who exactly are you after?"

"Four men. And if you could bring on David and Chris on this, I'd really appreciate it."

"Shelly, I'm not bringing on anybody until you tell me what's going on, and you haven't done that yet."

Lawson moved her head around. "I'm sorry. This whole thing just... I'm all over the place with it."

"What is this whole thing, as you keep saying?"

"A year ago, we had an assignment in Europe. I was part of the operation. It was big."

"They all are."

"This one involved a lot of players. Major players."

"In what racket?" Recker asked.

"Drugs, weapons, money laundering, you name it. It was so big we had to team up with MI6 on a joint task force."

"Happens. So what's the problem?"

"The problem is the operation failed."

"Also happens."

"But not like this. People got killed. Good people. Agents on both sides."

Recker was sympathetic, but still wasn't sure what this had to do with him. "So how does that lead us here?"

"I'm sorry. I guess I'm rambling. I just have so many thoughts swirling around in my head about all this, it's hard to get them straight."

Recker looked at his watch and smiled. "Well, looks like I've got some time, so... just try not to make it too long."

Lawson took a deep breath to collect her thoughts. "OK. So there was a major operation between us and MI6."

"I got that part."

Lawson gave him an eye. "Are you gonna let me finish?"

Recker smirked and threw his hands up. "I'm sorry. Proceed."

"So, anyway, there was this big operation. Long story short, the whole operation got screwed up, failed miserably, and two agents got killed. One of ours, and one from MI6."

"Like I said, it happens."

"It doesn't happen to me. I've spent a lot of time as a handler, and now that I've moved up in rank, I take a lot of pride in getting things right, and not getting people killed."

"Shelly, in this business, things can get screwed up in a hundred different ways, and none of them reflect on you in any way. It's the business. Just because something goes wrong doesn't mean someone's at fault. It's just the way it is."

"You know how many people have told me that in the last year?"

"Not enough, apparently."

"Mike, I'm not a rookie. I know things happen out there. I can accept that things go sideways sometimes. Like you said, it's part of the game. But what I can't accept is when there's a traitor in the mix. And that's what we're dealing with here."

"Traitor? How do you know?"

"A few weeks ago I got a tip from a source detailing everything that went wrong on that mission and why."

"And that source told you the mission was blown up from within?"

"Yes. And it happened on the MI6 side."

"They had a mole?"

"Apparently so."

"So it seems fairly simple, then. Call MI6, present them with the info, and let it fall where it may."

"If only it were that simple," Lawson said.

"Why isn't it?"

"Because the mole is no longer there."

"So put an alert out and move on. I'm not seeing the issue."

"The issue is that he's here in the United States."

Recker shrugged. "So pick him up. Or alert the FBI or whoever else you're in bed with these days."

"There's, of course, problems with that too."

"Such as?"

"One, we don't know where he is. We just know that he's here somewhere."

"And the others?" Recker asked, getting the picture there was more than one issue.

"I've been told not to pursue it."

"What?"

"I've been fighting the brass on this for weeks," Lawson said. "They're not budging. They've told me to stand down."

"Why?"

"That's just it, I don't know. None of it makes sense. I've been fighting tooth and nail on this and I haven't made one stitch of progress on it. And I'm not going to. They've told me to forget it and move on to other matters. They've literally put twenty other folders on my desk to make sure that I do."

"They're squeezing you out."

"Yes. What I can't figure out is why. We lost an agent on this. You'd think they'd want to put every resource available to find this guy. But instead they're just letting it pass like it was nothing."

"Listen, I know you're not a rookie," Recker said. "You've got a lot of experience, you've done a lot of things, and you're obviously very highly thought of. If not, they never would have let you deal with me."

"There's a but coming on, isn't there? I can feel it."

"But, sometimes you gotta learn when to walk away."

"Feels a little funny coming from you. Do you always walk away?"

Recker laughed. "I didn't say you should always follow my advice. Or that I always even followed it myself."

"Look, there's obviously something funny going on here. There was a mole in MI6, who got one of our agents killed, and now we have it on good authority that he's here in the US, and we're not going to do a thing about it."

"What's the guy here for?"

Lawson shrugged. "Who knows? Could be any of a

thousand reasons. Money, drugs, setting up a shipment, making a deal, could be anything."

"And what exactly do you want me to do?"

"I want you to find him."

"You don't have any FBI or local law enforcement contacts that could do that for you?"

"Like we keep saying, it's not that simple."

"So simplify it for me," Recker said.

"Because I want you to find him… and kill him."

2

Recker got to the office, finding Jones in his usual spot, typing away. They greeted each other, then Recker started pacing around the room. It didn't take long before Jones stopped what he was doing, noticing his friend's behavior.

"What is it this time?"

Recker stopped and looked at him. "What?"

"You're pacing."

Recker looked down at the floor. "Oh. I really need to change up my mannerisms."

"No, don't do that. I don't have another five years to figure out whatever you come up with next. Let's just stick to the status quo."

"Oh, well, if you insist."

"So should we talk about what's on your mind, or do you want to walk around the room for another twenty minutes stewing over it first?"

"I don't always do that."

"No, sometimes it's thirty."

Recker rolled his eyes. He looked around, noticing the absence of one of his partners. "Where's Chris?"

"He's home."

"What's the matter?"

"Nothing. There is nothing pressing going on, so I told him to stay home and rest up. No need for him to be here right now."

"Can't keep doing that, David."

"What?"

"He's healed, he says he's good, and he thinks he's ready. Don't sideline him."

"I just... want to make sure we don't put him back out too soon."

"Is this about him being ready, or about you being nervous to potentially put him in a dangerous position again?"

Jones made a face, like his partner had hit a sore spot. He looked down at the desk. "Maybe a little bit of both."

"If he says he's ready, you gotta take him at his word. If he says he's good, and you bench him, you risk alienating a star player and making him unhappy."

"This isn't baseball, Mike. It's not like he'd ask for a trade."

"How do you know? We don't operate on contracts here. If he doesn't feel valued, he'll go somewhere else where he does."

"He knows he's valued."

"Then show him," Recker said. "By all accounts, he's ready to go. Take the leash off."

Jones sighed, then nodded. He knew Recker was right. Maybe he was trying to mask his own insecurities. He just didn't want to make the same mistake again. But as his friend so aptly pointed out, none of them were rookies. Jones had to have faith in the judgment of his partners, as well as his own.

"I'll bring him back in as soon as we have something."

"Might be sooner than you think," Recker said.

Jones gave him a glance. His partner obviously knew something that he didn't. "Am I right to assume that we have something on the docket that I'm not aware of?"

"You should know me by now. It's never safe to assume anything."

"True. But I do get the impression I'm about to be hit with something out of left field."

"Not as much as I was."

"What exactly are we talking about here?" Jones asked.

"I got hit with a proposition a little while ago."

"Does Mia know?"

Now it was Recker's turn to give the dirty look. "Not that type of proposition."

"Well you didn't specify."

Recker then spent the next few minutes going over

everything he and Lawson talked about. Jones looked stunned.

"Why do you look like that?" Recker asked.

"Like what?"

"Like that. Like you can't believe it."

"Probably because I can't. Did you actually agree to any of this?"

"Haven't agreed to anything. After she told me about wanting to kill them, I just said I had to talk to you guys about it first. Wanted to run it past you, see what you thought, take it from there."

"This is kind of a bombshell," Jones said.

"You're telling me."

"Why did she come to you?"

"I thought I explained that? She wants to pursue it, she's getting put on the sidelines, and we're the only option."

"And we're supposed to suddenly find a double agent lurking somewhere within the borders? Just like that?"

"Well, I assume it's not going to be *that* easy," Recker replied. "But for someone like you, probably shouldn't take more than a few hours."

Jones let out a fake laugh. "Oh, yeah, just a few." He put his elbow on the desk and his hand on his chin. "I don't even know what to think. What do you think?"

"Honestly? I don't know either."

"We should probably bring Chris in on this. Did she say what she was offering for us to do this?"

"Again, I didn't ask for anything. She didn't offer anything. Should we?"

"I don't know. I mean, we did before."

"Before we get into all that, I think the main point we have to all agree on is do we really want to? Do we want to do this?"

"There is one small difference from the last time," Jones said.

"What's that?"

"This one isn't actually sponsored by the CIA. This one is off the books."

Recker let out a sigh and nodded. "Yeah. And if they find out we're on this, there's no telling how it's gonna go."

"Which begs the question, why are they standing down on this? You worked there. If an agent goes down, isn't it a priority to get closure on it? Wouldn't they want to wrap this up?"

"Not if there's something bigger in play."

"Such as?"

"Such as they're still wanting the guy to live for the time being for some other purpose," Recker said. "Could be he has access to a higher value target. Could be they're waiting for him to make contact with someone else that they want. Or…"

"Or what?"

"Or there could be some interagency crap going on."

"All of which makes me think we should maybe

leave it alone. I assume the CIA knows what it's doing."

Recker laughed. "I wouldn't put too much money on that one." He pointed to himself. "Case in point."

"True."

"And it could just be that they're stretched thin enough and they've got other things to work on that they put more value on."

"I'm still inclined to let it pass." As Jones watched Recker pace around the room, he could tell his partner had other ideas. "I'm assuming, which I know is dangerous with you, but I'm assuming that you do not share my opinion."

Recker stopped and looked at him. "Hmm? Oh, no, probably not."

"You're inclined to help, aren't you?"

Recker sighed. "Yeah. I guess I am."

"Can I ask why?"

"Because I don't think Lawson would ask to bring us in on this unless it was truly important, or there were no other options."

"Would you agree to this if it was someone other than her asking?"

"I don't know. Maybe not. But it is her asking. And she's done right by us since we've known her."

"I can't argue with that. I'm just not sure these are the right circumstances."

"Are there ever really right circumstances in our business?"

"Yes," Jones said, without hesitation.

"I'm not sure about that. You wanna call Chris, let him be the deciding vote?"

"I'm not sure we need a deciding vote. I'm not so dead set against it that I don't want to do it if that's what you want. I'm just giving my opinion. If you want to plow ahead with this, I'll be on board."

"Should still give Chris a say." Recker grabbed his phone and called Haley, who picked up right away. Recker could tell by that that he was itching to get back already. "Have the phone by your side waiting for something?"

"Yes!" Haley replied. "I'm tired of sitting here. I'm good. I'm ready. Please tell me you have something for me."

Recker laughed. "Maybe. We've got an offer from Michelle Lawson about doing another job for her."

"I'll take it! I don't care where, or the details, I'm in!"

Recker continued laughing. "Um, OK, well, I should probably just tell you about it first, though."

"Don't matter. I'm in."

"Sure you don't wanna know the details?"

"Fine, you can tell me, but it won't make any difference."

"Well, let me just explain what I know so far." Recker then let him know the details.

Just like Haley told him, it didn't make any difference. "I'm in. What do you think?"

"I'm inclined to say yes."

Split Scope

"Great, let's get on it. I can be in the office in twenty minutes and we can start nailing these clowns."

"Um, well, that might be a little premature. I still have to talk to Lawson again, let her know we'll take it."

"I can come in anyway. Get a jump start on things."

"OK, well, take your time."

"I will. Twenty minutes."

Recker let out another laugh as he hung up.

"Judging from your conversation, I take it Chris is in, as well?" Jones asked.

"That's an understatement."

"He's itching to get back."

"I think you could have told him we were going back in time to The Alamo, and he would have jumped at it."

"Well, if you were able to bring your gun cabinet with you, you could change the course of history."

Recker smiled. "Yeah." His phone then rang again. He initially assumed it was Haley again, hurrying things along, but it wasn't. It was a number he didn't recognize. "Hello?"

"Hi," Lawson said. "Me again."

"New phone?"

"Oh, no, just didn't want to be calling you from my regular number, just in case there are... well, you know."

Recker cleared his throat. "Certainly nobody we know would listen in or track your movements or anything."

"Oh, yeah, no. Nobody at all."

"I assume you have a reason for calling?"

"Sure do. Just wanted to see if you guys had kicked around my proposal yet?"

"We have."

"So? What do you think?"

"Right now we're likely to say yes." He could hear the happiness in her voice.

"That's great. I really appreciate it."

"Except."

"Except? Except what?" She suddenly got worried.

"We need to hear more details about everything. You only gave me a brief summary earlier. Now I need the in-depth version."

"Fine. I can give you everything you need."

"OK, let's set up a time to meet," Recker said.

"How about now?"

"Uh, yeah, I guess that could work."

"Great, I could meet you and David at the same time."

"Both of us?"

"Well you're both in, aren't you?"

Recker looked at Jones. "Yeah, I guess so."

"Great. Be right there."

"Wait, what? Be right where?"

"I'll meet you at the office," Lawson said.

"You'll do what now?"

"Meet you at the office. Surely you didn't forget that I know where you are, right?"

"Uh, no, I didn't."

Lawson smiled. "Why don't you walk over to the window."

Recker briefly looked at Jones, then at the window. He already knew what he was going to find. He walked over to it, then looked out. He immediately saw Lawson standing there in the parking lot, leaning against the hood of her car. She looked up at him and waved. Recker returned the motion, though he only gave a half-hearted wave.

"David."

"Yes?"

"Were you in the mood for meeting Lawson now?"

Jones looked up at him. "Right now?"

"Unless you're too busy."

"No, I suppose I could swing it if it's necessary. Why does she need both of us, though?"

Recker shrugged. "Beats me. I guess she'll tell us when she gets here."

Jones stopped typing. "Here?"

Recker pointed out the window. "She's here."

Jones instantly jumped out of his chair and hurried over to the window. He looked out and saw Lawson, who also gave him a wave. Jones gave the same half-hearted wave in return.

"What is she doing here?" Jones asked.

Recker smiled. "Like I said... guess she'll tell us."

3

There was a knock on the door. In any other instance, Recker and Jones would have been startled, knowing they weren't expecting anyone. Nobody ever knocked on the door. It was only the three people that belonged there, and Mia, occasionally. This would be a new experience.

Recker and Jones looked at each other. Recker put his arm up in the direction of the door.

"Well aren't you gonna answer it?"

Jones stared at him. "It's your friend."

"It's technically your office since you own it."

"You invited her."

"I didn't invite her."

"The door, Michael?"

Recker huffed and puffed, but went over to the door and opened it. Lawson walked in. Recker took a quick peek outside, just to make sure she was alone and didn't bring any agency friends. There was nobody else there, though.

Lawson walked in, looking around the place like she was inspecting it the way she would a new apartment, or looking for a house. She seemed pleased with it.

"Very nice."

Jones smiled. "It suits our purposes."

"I've always thought this was an ingenious setup. I mean, having this overtop of a laundromat was a stroke of genius."

Jones looked happy to hear that. "Well, it was my idea." Recker rolled his eyes at hearing Jones boast.

"Nobody would ever think of looking here."

Jones kept smiling. "All part of the plan." He clasped his hands together in front of him. "Speaking of the plan, this isn't ever going to become a regular thing, is it? Not that you're not welcome, but it's other people who... who else knows about this, anyway?"

"About me being here? No one."

"No, I mean, about us being here at all."

"Oh," Lawson said. "Uh, a few. You don't have anything to worry about. We work at the CIA. We're good at keeping secrets."

"Yes, I'm aware."

"Really, you don't have anything to worry about. You don't have to pack up and move. Wouldn't do you any good, anyway."

"Why is that?"

"We'd just find you again."

Jones raised an eyebrow. "How reassuring."

Recker walked past Lawson and directed her to the couch. "You can probably sit over here."

"Thanks," Lawson said, sitting down. "I'm sorry for dropping in like this. I'm sure this is probably a little uncomfortable for both of you, me being here like this in your... space."

Recker sat down next to her. "Not uncomfortable for us, right David?"

"Well, maybe slightly for me," Jones replied.

"I'm sorry," Lawson said. "It's just... since I knew you guys were here anyway, I didn't figure it really mattered, and it would save a lot of time."

"It certainly does that."

Lawson looked around. "Chris isn't here?"

"Oh, he's on his way in," Recker answered. "Another fifteen minutes probably."

"Oh. Good. So you're all in agreement on this?"

"You really didn't give me a lot of details yet."

Lawson reached into her pocket and pulled out a flash drive. She handed it to Recker. "Everything you need should be on here. At least to get you started."

"Is this everything you've got?"

"Everything. The details of the mission in England that went sideways, everything we have on Logan Harris, and the people we believe he's here with now."

"Harris is the former MI6 agent?"

"Yes."

"Did you ever deal with him personally?" Recker asked.

"No."

"Before I agree to anything, you need to come clean on this."

"What? What do you mean?"

"There's gotta be more to it than just avenging a former colleague. I'm not a rookie either."

Lawson took a deep breath. "OK. You're right. The agent we lost was a good friend of mine."

"Boyfriend?"

"No. Just a friend. A good one. And a good agent. And I can't just sit back and let Harris walk away when I have good intel that he's here and we can do something about it."

"You care too much," Recker said.

"Just like you do."

Recker grinned. "Yeah."

"Anyway, it looks like Harris and his three cronies came in last week through New York. Where they went after that is anyone's guess. I've done some preliminary work to try and track them down, but it's gone nowhere so far. And like I said, my case load's going through the roof, so it's not something I can continue pursuing on my own."

"We can look into it."

"I really appreciate it."

Jones still had more questions, though. "There is still the matter of what we're supposed to do with these people when we find them. If we find them. You say Harris has three other people he's working with?"

"At least. I've identified the three other men. They're in the file. They're all former MI6 agents. Two of them were washed out, and the other two, including Harris, quit on their own."

"So they're all obviously dangerous," Recker said.

"Yes. And they're not afraid to kill."

"This could be a very tricky situation," Jones said. "It could be way bigger than just these four."

"I know it."

"What if these four are just a small piece in a very large puzzle? What if there are international criminal organizations involved here? There could be a lot of pieces getting moved around the game board."

"I'm well aware."

"Just how far are we expected to take this?"

"As far as you can," Lawson replied. "Or as far as you want to. If you find these four, and you just want to take them out and be done with it, that's a win in my book. And if you get to them, and find the trail goes on much deeper than just them, and you want to pursue that, you can."

"Are we supposed to take everyone out beyond them?"

Lawson shrugged. "I expect you guys to use your best judgment. Whatever you feel the situation calls for."

"We're getting a lot of leeway on this," Recker said.

"Yes. Like I said, you're doing this for me, so there's no one else in play."

"And what if we stumble into something that eventually winds up being something that the CIA is already investigating? Another operation or something."

Lawson smiled. "Well, since you're doing this on your own, there's really no heat that can get put on any of us from the agency's perspective."

"And if we find Harris and the others and put a bullet in them?"

"Then we walk away, wiping our hands, knowing the situation's over."

"And if it turns out to be something bigger than any of us think?"

"Then we'll cross that bridge when we come to it. If at any point you want to walk away, I'll understand. Whether you find Harris or not."

Recker looked away for a second, obviously thinking about something. The look was not lost on the others.

"What is it?" Lawson asked.

"I can tell you right now this is probably more complicated than it seems."

"I know that."

"If it was as simple as just taking out a former agent who killed one of ours, he'd already be in handcuffs. Or dead."

"I agree."

"So the fact that he's not indicates there is something larger at play here."

"But what if there's not? What if there's some pressure from MI6, or other officers in the CIA, who just want the matter done with? Maybe they're afraid to look further, afraid they might find more that they don't like."

Recker rubbed his chin as he thought about it. "Well, one thing's for sure, no matter what the answer is, as soon as you go down the rabbit hole, there's no telling what you might find. And it could go in any number of directions."

"I know."

Recker looked at her and could see that this was an important matter for her. If it was someone other than her bringing it to him, he probably wouldn't be so willing, or eager, to jump at it. And he still wasn't, really. But seeing that it was her, and he felt some loyalty to her, all the way back to when she got him out of that situation when the CIA captured him, he was inclined to help her whenever she needed it.

"I'll take this as far as I can."

Lawson smiled, grabbing his arm. "Thank you. There is one other thing I wanted to bring up."

"Yeah?"

"I know whenever we've worked together before, there was an exchange of favors. There's nothing I can really do on this. At least officially."

"We get it."

"I mean, since this is off the books, there's nothing I can run up the chain for you."

"I'm not asking."

"I know, but I just wanted to say it. That doesn't mean that if you ever need something in the future that you can't come to me. I'd like to think we've moved past the stage where we're only doing things for a future favor."

"Noted."

"So, even though there's nothing I can technically give you for this, if the situation ever arises in the future where you need me... just ask."

Recker smiled. "I'll keep it in mind."

They continued talking about everything for the next little while, the mission in England, Harris, the agent that was lost, and suspicions about what Harris and his cohorts were really doing in the United States now. As they did, Haley finally made an appearance. He walked through the door, stunned upon seeing Lawson sitting there on the couch, directly in front of him.

"Hey, Chris," she greeted.

Haley was frozen, about halfway between the door and her. "Uh, did I walk into another dimension or something?"

"I doubt it," Recker answered.

"Or did I take some kind of experimental hallucinogenic CIA drug?"

Everyone in the room laughed. "Not hardly," Jones said.

"I'm in the right place?"

"I would say so."

"Are we just letting anyone walk in here nowadays?"

"We were thinking about it," Recker replied. "Maybe turn this place into some type of computer station or game station for those who are getting their clothes washed downstairs."

Jones literally shivered at the thought.

"I was already in the neighborhood," Lawson said. "Figured I'd just stop in and give you all the lowdown on what was going on."

"Oh, the case," Haley said. "What's going on with that?"

"I'll fill you in," Recker answered.

"OK, well, I should probably be going," Lawson said, standing up. "Like I said, everything we have is on that file. Take a look, and if there's anything you don't understand, or need clarification on, just give me a call."

"We'll do that."

"Just, um, call me on that other number. Not on my regular one. You know how it is."

Recker smiled. "I do. Gotta keep everything off the books."

Lawson walked over to the door. "I guess I should also add that I'm not throwing you into the dark on this. While you're not getting agency support, you're still getting mine. So if there's anything you need, something you need me to run down that you can't get yourselves, just let me know. I'll do what I can."

"Always good to know," Jones said. "We will do that."

Lawson then left. Haley looked at the others and clapped his hands. "So, what'd I miss?"

Recker shook his head at him. "You're so itching to come back, aren't you?"

"You know it."

"You're sure you're ready?" Jones asked.

"If I was any more ready, I'd be unready." Haley made an expression like even he wasn't sure what he just said. "See? I'm so ready I'm not even making sense."

The others laughed at him. Recker held the flash drive in his hand. He stood up.

"Well, let's take a look and see what's on here."

4

The team spent several hours looking over, and discussing, the information compiled on Logan Harris. It was all compelling. None of it was promising.

Jones threw his hands up. "What are we supposed to do with this?"

Recker took his eyes off his computer and looked at his partner. "Track him down?"

"Yes, but how?"

"Isn't that usually your department?"

"All we know is he's somewhere on the East Coast," Jones replied. "He arrived in New York. His conspirators all arrived on different flights. One in Boston. One in Baltimore. One in Newark. There's been no trace of any of them since they got here. We don't know if they're together, they're separate, what their plans are, where they're at now, nothing. They've just disappeared off the map."

"Why do you say all this like it's something of a surprise? Did you think you were going to find them all eating the triple pancake breakfast at Denny's or something?"

"Of course not. I thought I would have something to locate them with, though. A thimble, a thread, the proverbial needle in the haystack. Not only do we not have a needle, we don't even have the haystack."

"First off, David, I haven't heard of anyone under the age of one-fifty talking about a thimble. I'm pretty sure that word went out of style along with covered wagons and stagecoaches."

Jones glared at him. "Are we really going to take offense to my choice of words when you know the intent behind them?"

"Well I'm just saying that if you want to make a comparison, you should make one with more of a recency bias. I mean, I'm betting that ninety-five percent of the population doesn't even know what a thimble is."

Jones tapped his fingers on the desk. "I sincerely hope that you're enjoying yourself."

Recker smiled. "Well, maybe a smidgeon."

Haley laughed. "These are the moments that I miss the most."

Jones continued tapping on the desk. "Are we done now?"

Recker shrugged. "I guess."

"As I was saying, there is not one shred of evidence

pointing us in any direction. Though the case against Harris appears rock-solid, and it seems obvious that he is guilty of what he's been charged with, there's not even a guess as to what he's here for. Or where he is. Or who he's doing business with."

"Well maybe if you stopped being a negative Nelly, and we actually used our investigative skills and searched for them, perhaps we might find them. Don't you think?"

"And what are we supposed to search with?"

Recker looked at him strangely. "Is this a different David that we're dealing with today? Did you clone yourself and forget to add the brain part to this one? How do we usually start running people down? Follow the trail. Phone records, credit cards, social media, text messages, camera footage. Any of that ring a bell?"

"All of which could have been done already. If they found anything, it would be in the file."

"It hasn't been done."

"How do you know?"

"Because, as Lawson told us, nobody else is looking for them. Are you just stalling because you didn't wanna take this on?"

"No, I'm not stalling," Jones said. "Maybe I'm just off my groove today."

Recker grinned. "Well we all have our moments, don't we?"

Jones sighed, then started acting like his usual self. He started using his facial recognition software, most of which was a carbon copy of the NSA's system, with a few wrinkles of his own in there. While that was running, he also started his search for their names, and any known aliases, to see if anything came up regarding phone records, credit card statements, or just regular internet activity.

"Not surprisingly, these guys have very little footprint anywhere," Jones said, typing away.

"So they're basically us," Haley said.

Recker looked at him and nodded. "These guys are good. They know how to stay off the grid. They know how to move undetected."

"Except at airports," Jones said. He then looked confused.

It was a look not lost on Recker. "What is it?"

"Think about it. We're talking these guys up about how good they are, and they certainly seem to be, but all four were spotted at airports coming in. Why is that? Wouldn't they have devised a plan to slip in undetected? Sure, they've disappeared since then, but why let yourself be known at all?"

Recker and Haley looked at each other, neither having a good answer. There was only one reason that could be, though.

"Because they wanted to be," Recker said.

Haley nodded, agreeing with the assessment. "Absolutely."

"What?" Jones asked.

"They wanted to be spotted," Recker answered.

"Well that just doesn't make a lick of sense. Why would you let yourself be spotted, and then promptly disappear like you didn't want anyone to find you?"

"Because they didn't."

Jones scratched the side of his face, looking confused. "What?"

"They didn't want to be found."

"But you just said they wanted to be spotted."

"They did," Recker said.

Jones put his hand on his forehead. "Good Lord. And I thought I was out of sorts today."

"Mike's right," Haley said. "They came in, wanted someone to know they were here, then disappeared, not wanting anyone else to find them."

Jones still had a confused look on his face. "Let me get this straight. You're saying they wanted someone, we don't know who, to spot them, letting them know these guys were here? But then they disappeared, so nobody could find them?"

"That's the size of it."

Jones shook his head, still not thinking that made one bit of sense. He then started mumbling. "It must be a CIA thing."

"No, let me explain it," Recker said.

"Oh, please do." Jones pushed his chair away from the desk so he could focus on what his friend was saying to hopefully understand better.

Recker grinned, knowing what he was saying wasn't making much sense to his partner. But it made sense to him. "So, these guys are under the radar for most of the world. They slip in here, and want someone specific to know they're here. They let themselves be seen, so that party knows they're here. Then they disappear so the authorities can't trace them."

"But now the other party knows they're here, they can start putting the feelers out to start doing business," Haley said.

Jones shook his head. "None of that makes any sense. If they're doing business with this third party, why not just contact them directly? Let them know they're coming. Set up a meeting. Why go through the charade?"

"Couple reasons," Recker answered. "One, this way keeps them in control."

"How so?"

"If you're not especially trusting, then you don't contact the people you're doing business with directly, because you don't trust that they're not being watched, followed, phones tapped, listening devices, and so on."

"This way, you control it," Haley said. "When they contact you, you control the environment, how contact is made."

Jones's eyes darted to one of his partners, then to the other. He then scratched the top of his head. "But if they're waiting for contact to be made, all those concerns would still be valid, would they not?"

Recker shook his head. "Not if you do it right. Contact isn't made directly at first. They'd use a neutral party for the initial contact. Then, Harris and his group would set up the parameters for making contact directly from that point on."

Jones put his finger across his lip as he tried to understand. "So to put this in terms I can wrap my head around, let's just say I'm Harris."

"That's a stretch."

"OK, let's say you're Harris, and I want to make a deal with you."

"Right."

"I wouldn't come to you directly at first."

"No. Well, I mean, you could, I guess. But that requires some faith on the part of both groups. And if you haven't done business before, might not be a good idea."

"And even if you have," Haley said. "If things didn't go perfectly before, you might still be wary."

"OK," Jones said. "So say you and I have never done business before. I see you're in the area, and I want to contact you. Instead of coming to you, because I don't know where you are, I go to Chris. Then he goes to you, and tells you of my interest. Then you tell him you are, and how we communicate from there. Is that about right?"

Recker nodded. "That's the size of it. Because I know I'm wanted, I tell you how and where we'll meet, what the conditions and terms are, everything. I control it. That way I know there's no chance of anything going wrong on your end."

"Until whenever money has exchanged hands, or whatever else they're trading." Jones rubbed his eyes. "Another thing, if I go to Chris to find you, how do I know he can actually make contact with you? How will he find you?"

"Well, for the purposes of this exercise, we've dumbed it down quite a bit. In reality, there's going to be a lot more pieces in play. You and I would most likely already have some mutual friends in common who have already floated our names in the air to the other. In that case, we'll have several people who already know both parties. I might have Chris' number and contact him to let him know I'm in town. Then when he receives word from you, then we'll find each other."

"Sounds like it's overcomplicating things to me," Jones said.

"Well, like I said, it depends on how trusting, or paranoid, you are. If you're extremely either of those things, you'll go to a lot of trouble to try and control things as much as possible."

"And it's equally possible that it's none of the things you've just said."

Recker shrugged. "Possible. Until we have something more concrete to go on, all we can do is guess."

"Have you participated in schemes like this while you worked for the agency?" Jones asked.

"Well, you often have to go through a third party

for information, or to retrieve something, or whatever. It's just part of the game."

"Sounds like a dumb part."

"Not if you don't wanna get caught or killed."

"And these guys don't want either," Haley said.

"So how are we going to drill this down?" Jones asked.

"First, we need to catch a break," Recker answered. "Find out a location, a name, something. Once we get that first bit, the ball will start rolling, then we can begin to pin it down further. We just need that first break."

5

Recker was sitting at the table, waiting for Vincent to arrive. While Jones and Haley continued working the computers on their end, using whatever technology that was at their disposal, Recker wanted to take a different approach. It'd been three days since they officially had taken the case from Lawson, and while that wasn't an especially long period of time, Recker didn't want to just sit on his hands and wait.

There was no guarantee that his partners would find something. Vincent had a lot of connections. Connections to a particular group of people who might actually have business with the likes of Harris and his crew. But even if Vincent didn't know anything about the situation yet, he might know who would. It was worth a try.

It was one of the few times Recker had beaten

Vincent to the diner. Vincent was almost always at the table waiting for him, usually about to finish a plate of something. Recker took the liberty of ordering, knowing what Vincent liked. Vincent, and his entourage, arrived about ten minutes later. Malloy, and a couple other men, swept the room like they usually did, making sure there were no unfriendly faces already seated somewhere, waiting to take a shot at him.

Vincent, seeing Recker already seated at their regular table, zoomed past his men and took a seat. His food was already on the table. Vincent sat across from Recker, looked down at his food, then gave Recker a smile.

"Have I really become this predictable?"

Recker grinned and shrugged. "Maybe I'm just a really observant man?"

"Let's settle on maybe both points being true."

"Fair enough."

Vincent started digging into his food. "Still warm."

"Took the liberty of assuming you were getting here soon."

"I apologize for my tardiness." Vincent looked at his watch. "Ten minutes late. Unforgivable."

"Happens."

"I pride myself on punctuality. No self-respecting business should run without it. But, as you say, things do come up."

"Hopefully nobody got hurt in the process," Recker said with a smile.

Vincent laughed. "Ah, you know I don't prefer the violent method." He then gave a tug to his suit jacket. "Besides, this is one of my best suits. I'd hate to get blood on this thing."

"Clothes make the man, right?"

"So they say. Now that we've gotten the obligatory small talk out of the way, what's this all about?"

"Business."

Vincent smiled. "Isn't it always?"

"This is... different."

"How so?"

"We're looking for people."

Vincent smiled again. "As I said, aren't we always?"

"As I said... this time is different."

"We seem to be going around in circles."

"Logan Harris. Know him?"

Vincent turned his head, looking like he was giving the question some thought. "No. Don't believe I do. Why? Friend of yours?"

"Hardly. He's an ex-MI6 agent. Apparently he's here somewhere."

"Interesting. I'm not sure what you're doing here talking to me, though. Shouldn't you be meeting with the CIA, or FBI, or one of those other crackpot agencies?"

"It's a little more difficult than that," Recker replied. "Look, I don't wanna bother you with all the boring details, so I'll just get down to the meat of it. Harris, and three guys, all ex-agents, are here somewhere. I'm trying to track them down."

"Why?"

Recker lifted his hand off the table, as if he were shrugging with it. "Let's just say it's a favor to someone."

"You say somewhere. Somewhere in the city or somewhere in the country?"

"We believe they're on the East Coast."

"Well that narrows it down. Why don't you tell me exactly what this is about? Unless it's a matter of national security or something."

"It just might be."

"If I'm to help you on this, whatever it might be, I need names, dates, places, and whatever else you can tell me."

Recker took out a piece of paper from his pocket and put it on the table. Vincent picked it up and read the four names.

"So these are the four James Bond wannabees?" Vincent asked.

"They're dangerous men. We don't know exactly what they're doing here. Could be drugs, maybe it's weapons, maybe it's some highly classified information or something. Just don't know at this point."

"And why is this a concern of yours? Or mine, to be more frank?"

"They've killed an American citizen. That makes it our business, no?"

Vincent shrugged. He didn't necessarily see it the same way. "Noble, maybe. Our business? Maybe not."

"I'm doing this as a favor for someone who's a friend. That person that was killed was their friend. And whatever these guys are doing... it's not good. And they need to be stopped."

"And, pardon the pun, you'll do the silencing?"

"If it's necessary."

"Just what is it that you think I can do to help?"

"You know people," Recker answered. "Whatever these guys are doing, you might have a connection to them."

"You haven't even told me where to look."

Recker sighed, knowing how far-fetched it all sounded. "They came in through four different airports. We know that much. Boston, New York, Newark, and Baltimore. Then they disappeared."

Vincent laughed. "Sounds like something right out of a movie."

Recker tilted his head and made a face, not disagreeing with the assessment. "Listen, I don't usually try to pry into your business, as long as it doesn't affect me. But whatever these guys are here for, maybe what they're doing affects your business."

"Taking business that might eventually come my way, that's what you're implying?"

"Who knows? Maybe."

"Trying to appeal to my pocketbook, huh?"

"Whatever works."

"This is big, isn't it? Bigger than you or me."

Recker looked away for a second. "Could be. I'll be honest. I don't know exactly what we're up against, or what we'll find. Maybe we'll find they're just a bunch of guys looking to set up their own operation here. Or maybe we'll find out they're pawns in a much bigger operation that spans a bunch of different operators or countries. Whatever the case, once I go down this road, there's no turning back."

Vincent took a sip of his drink as he thought about it. "Pardon me if I'm wrong, but isn't this a government problem?"

"Should be."

"So why aren't they involved? Or are they?"

"If they're involved, I don't know about it. Now, whether they're keeping it hush-hush, or they're just being oblivious, that's a matter for another day. And there's no guarantee we won't run into them once we get into this."

"So what you're saying is that any of my inquiries should be kept on the down low?"

"I would say that's a good idea."

Vincent put his hand over his mouth as he deliberated. He didn't get a chance to answer, as Malloy walked down to the table. He patted Recker on the shoulder, then leaned over and whispered something in Vincent's ear. Vincent glanced up at him, not having much of an expression on his face. He wiped his mouth with a napkin. He then stood up.

"Excuse me, Mike, I have another matter that I have to attend to." Recker waved his hand and nodded. Vincent stood at the edge of the table, not yet leaving, as he continued to think about the proposition. He then pointed to the paper with the names. "May I take that with me?"

Recker picked it up and handed it to him. "Of course."

"Thank you. I'll see what I can do. I can make no promises."

"I understand."

"But I'll do my best for you."

"I appreciate that."

Vincent left to attend to his business, Malloy right behind him, who tapped Recker on the arm again as they left. Recker turned and watched them leave the diner, then stared out the window. He wasn't sure how much help Vincent would be able to give, but at least it was a start.

Back at the office, Recker entered, noticing Jones and Haley sitting next to each other, both on computers. The fact that neither of them jumped up excitedly to greet him, eager to shower him with new information, told him they hadn't found out anything yet.

"Don't get up on my account," Recker said.

Jones smirked, but didn't turn around or look at him. "We're not."

"Should I assume we've still got no leads?"

"Aren't you the one that says you should never assume anything?"

"Am I?"

"Assumptions are dangerous in this business."

Recker slightly turned his head, looking at his friend out of the corner of his eye. He couldn't tell whether Jones was kidding him or not. "Wait, so you do have something?"

"No."

Recker sighed and rolled his eyes. "Thanks for that."

"Sorry. But you do say assumptions are dangerous."

"So is toying with someone's emotions." Recker was about to jab at his partner some more when his phone rang. He looked at the ID. It was Lawson. "It's Michelle. What am I supposed to tell her?"

"The truth usually works."

Recker answered the phone, then walked around the room as he talked. Jones leaned over to Haley.

"What do you think is really going on here?" Jones asked.

Haley looked at Recker. "I'd say that Lawson wants an update."

"No, not that. I mean, with this whole situation.

What do you think is really going on? There has to be more to it than we know."

"Usually is."

"I just find it hard to believe that the CIA would just let these people off the hook after what happened."

"My gut tells me that there's something bigger at play."

"But what?"

"These guys likely have ties to someone else," Haley said. "Someone the CIA wants more. It's probably as simple as that. Harris and his bunch can lead them there."

"But wouldn't Lawson know that?"

"Probably."

"And yet she still wants to take these guys out, even knowing that her employers want them alive for another purpose. Very strange. Seems like she's cutting off her nose to spit in their face."

"I don't think that's how the saying goes."

"You know what I mean."

"She might be having a disagreement about how important this crew is to whoever else they're after," Haley said. "She might think they're not necessary to the bigger group. Might think they can find or eliminate them without Harris and his boys. She might be concerned that even if they lead to this other group, Harris' crew will slip away and it'll be tough picking them up again. She might be concerned that the only time to hit this bunch is now."

"That's a lot of might's."

Haley smiled. "Might be."

"Even if what you're saying is true, she's playing a dangerous game with this. Going against her superiors."

"Well, technically she's not. We are."

"Just the same, she's the one bringing us in."

"Off books. None of this will come back to her. Now that we're talking about it, I'm willing to bet everything I just said is exactly how it is. It's the only thing that makes sense."

"Still seems like an awful big risk on her part," Jones said. "I mean, I fully get wanting to avenge something like that. Losing a friend. A colleague. It's tough. No doubt about it. But disobeying orders, especially for someone like her, seems against character."

"People disobey orders all the time. When you're out in the field, it's about survival."

"And I understand that. But she's not in the field on this."

Haley shrugged. "It is what it is."

"Does it potentially bother you that we might take these people out and possibly hurt a bigger operation? Maybe someone who is more important? Or a more evil individual, if you will?"

Haley answered immediately. "No."

"Why not?"

"Because there is always someone more evil out there. One of those in-the-field lessons that you find out real early. There's always someone or something worse."

"I guess I just worry about letting something worse slide because of our intervention."

"It's an understandable worry."

"But not one that you share?"

"I trust that Lawson's instincts are right on this. She's bright, she knows what's going on."

"And her superiors don't?"

Haley grinned. "People in charge don't always have the same position as those underneath them."

"Still seems risky for her to me."

"She'll be all right."

"Well, it may all be a moot point if we don't locate these people sometime soon."

They went back to work, as Recker continued talking on the phone. It was only a minute or two later when something popped up on Jones' screen. He stopped typing and stared at his monitor. He was somewhat surprised in that he really didn't think they'd get something at this point. It was a lead. An actual lead. Something they could pursue.

After a few more minutes, Recker's conversation finally ended. He turned around and started talking without really looking at his partners.

"Lawson doesn't have any more info for us." Recker started to talk more, but quickly stopped, seeing the face on Jones. "What? What is it? Why do you look like that?"

"Like what?" Jones asked.

Recker pointed at him. "Like that. Like you just won something. You look like you either just won the lottery, or you just found out about your surprise party."

Jones smiled. "Because we finally have something."

"Say what?"

"We're in business."

6

Recker rushed over to the desk to see what Jones was looking at. He saw the picture of Mac Webb on the screen, one of Logan Harris' accomplices.

"He's the number two man?" Recker said.

"Well, I think they are all number two men," Jones replied. "Harris is clearly one. Everyone else is behind him."

"Where was this taken?"

Jones put his finger on the screen, running it down from the top until he got to what he was looking for. "Baltimore."

"When?"

"Approximately six hours ago."

Recker folded his arms and stared at the screen. Jones started typing again, keeping the picture of Webb on the left side of the screen as he typed away on the right. Several other screens quickly flashed on that side of the monitor over the next minute or two.

"What are you doing?" Recker asked.

Jones pointed to Webb's picture again. "Look. He's in a car."

"Yeah, but we can't make out a make or anything."

"But we can see that he's driving, and there doesn't appear to be anyone else in the car with him."

"And?"

"And we know his location at that point and time. Now I'm expanding the search to see if any other nearby cameras picked up the vehicle after that."

"Wouldn't you have gotten an alert if they did?"

Jones shook his head. "I only put pictures of their faces in the program, because that's all we had to go on. We didn't have anything else for a camera to pick up. Now we have a vehicle. Now, we can only tell that it's a black sedan, but if there's another camera that picks up the car, even if they don't have a shot of Webb's face, we can start piecing things together."

"Maybe we can find the trail of where he's going," Haley said.

Seconds later, another alert sounded. Jones immediately pulled up what it was. "There we go. Another camera picked up the car."

Recker leaned in closer to get a better look. He pointed at the car. "Is that a license plate?"

Jones zoomed in. "That is a license plate. Looks like

a very good shot, too. All the numbers and letters are visible."

"Should be able to get something out of that."

"Let's see." Jones typed in the plate number. "Comes back to a fake name."

"Or a real name that's working with him."

"Could be. Looks like it is a rental."

"It's a place to start," Recker said. He started moving around as if he were about to leave.

"Where are you going?"

"Baltimore."

"But we don't have anything else yet."

"Well you keep working on it. We're not gonna get anywhere just staying here. Gotta go where the action is." He looked at Haley, who was still seated in the same spot, looking like he had something on his mind. "What is it?"

Haley looked at him. "Just strange."

"What is?"

"Webb arrived... what, last week?"

"Yeah."

"But he's still in Baltimore. Why? Now, either they're all in Baltimore, or they're still split up. And if that's the case, why haven't they gotten together yet?"

Recker looked at the wall for a second, thinking. "Either they've got multiple deals lined up in different cities, or... they don't have any deals lined up yet and they're still looking for someone."

"Or multiple people."

"That's gotta be it. Otherwise there'd be no reason to still be apart. We know they're a group, they're likely selling something together, that's the only reason they'd still be separated."

"Unless the others are down there with him," Jones said. "Which we still cannot confirm yet."

"We gotta get down there. They've been here for over a week, and I can guarantee you, that they're not gonna be here much longer."

"Why?"

"Four men who are wanted by a government agency arrive in the country of that agency. You really think they're comfortable sticking around here for weeks at a time?"

"No, I guess not."

"My hunch is that they're here for two weeks," Recker said. "Anything longer than that, I doubt they have much interest in staying. Either they gave themselves two weeks to find someone, or complete a deal, or get something rolling, then they're leaving."

Haley nodded, agreeing with the assessment. "Yeah, sounds about right. If it was me, I wouldn't stick around much longer than that."

"Which means we only have a couple of days left."

Jones went back to typing on his computer. "Before you go, let's see what else I can come up with here."

"No time. It's a two-hour drive, roughly. Whatever you get, you can text or call us."

"Might be good to book a hotel down there," Haley said. "That way we don't have to keep going back and forth."

Recker nodded, looking at Jones. "I'm on it," Jones said. "I'll let you know where."

Recker and Haley grabbed a couple of weapons from the cabinet, then headed toward the door.

"What about Mia?" Jones asked.

"I'll let her know where I'll be for the next few days. You just concentrate on getting that stuff."

"Yes, yes."

As Recker and Haley hit the road, Jones continued his digging into Mac Webb. First, he booked a hotel room for his partners for when they got to Baltimore. Then, he drilled down on Webb, and the name that was used to rent the car he was seen driving. Marci Johnson was the name Jones was looking for now. He got the feeling the name was legit, though. He doubted Webb used a fake name from the opposite gender. That wouldn't fool anybody. Jones just had to figure out the connection between Webb and Johnson.

It didn't take long, though. Jones was able to hack into the database of the rental car company pretty quickly. Once he was in, it didn't take much effort to find Johnson's name. He then started pulling up as much information as he could on her. After twenty minutes, he called Recker to let him know what he found out so far.

"Get something?" Recker asked.

"The name of the person who rented the car is Marci Johnson."

"Marci Johnson?" The tone of Recker's voice clearly indicated his surprise. "Who the hell's that?"

"Give me a moment and I'll tell you."

"Moment's up."

"Looks like she is thirty years old, spent a couple of years in jail under a burglary charge..."

"Sounds like a peach," Recker said. "How does she connect to Webb, though?"

"That's unclear so far. I can't find a connection yet."

"You sure it's a real person, and they didn't just forge some fake document?"

"Well, I'm looking at her driver's license, pulling up some other documents, social media..."

"How about a camera inside the car rental place?"

"Already checked," Jones answered. "They didn't have one. You didn't expect it to be that easy, did you?"

"Well I can hope."

"Wait, here's a social media page. Pictures on there match the driver's license."

"When was she last active on it?"

"Looks like yesterday. Going through some pictures now."

"While you're doing that, just give us her address and we'll head there, see if we can pick something up."

Jones texted him Johnson's address, then continued looking for that connection between her and Webb. Of course, there didn't have to be a connection between the two of them directly. They might have just had a mutual friend that brought them together. In that case, it would probably be tough to identify who that person was. But still, Jones stayed at it.

Jones kept looking for the next hour, not finding much that interested him. Everything he found out about Johnson painted the picture of a troubled woman, who fell in with the wrong crowd at an early age, and just couldn't seem to break free of it. Brushes with the law, drugs, and men that seemed to hurt more than help. It was the pattern that Johnson couldn't get out of.

Then, Jones found it. He found that link he was looking for. Pictures on one of her social media pages from two years ago. There was one of Webb and Johnson in the same shot, sitting next to each other at a table. Neither was looking at the camera. It appeared to be inside someone's house or apartment. There was an arm from someone else at the edge of the picture, but no other faces were seen. It could have been from a party. Or maybe just a few friends getting together. Whatever the case, it was clear proof that Webb and Johnson knew each other, and that Johnson was involved in this somehow. Jones called Recker again.

"We're just getting into Baltimore now," Recker said.

"Good. I found the connection."

"What is it?"

"A picture from two years ago. I'm sending it to your phone now. Webb and Johnson were sitting next to each other."

"Where?"

"I don't know."

"That means Webb's been here before," Recker said. "Or she's been to England."

"Nothing in her records indicates she's been out of the country before. She doesn't even own a passport."

"So Webb's been here, then. But that's not in his file either."

"There's a lot we don't know about all of this," Jones replied. "I would say it's likely that this is not this group's first visit here. And considering it's not documented in the file that Lawson gave us, I'd say they might not know of his previous visits either."

"They romantically involved?"

"Tough to say just from this photo. I haven't uncovered anything else, either a picture, or otherwise. Not a lot to go on."

"It's enough," Recker said.

"What are you going to do?"

"I think it's time we have a conversation with Ms. Johnson."

"Do you think that's wise? They obviously have some sort of relationship. And considering her name's on the rental, it's likely that they've been in contact recently. Without knowing where he is, she could contact him, let him know we're on to him, and spook him permanently."

"That's what I'd be counting on."

"Would you like to repeat that? You want Webb to get spooked? Doesn't that run counter to our whole point here?"

"If we start leaning on Johnson, and asking questions about Webb, she'll obviously immediately let him know."

"And?"

"Can't you trace the call?"

"Yes."

"Then there you go."

"What if I can't?"

"Then we'll figure something else out," Recker answered.

"It's a risk."

"Well we don't have time to just sit outside her place for a few days and watch her, hoping that she meets up with Webb somehow. Their business together might be finished. They might not meet again. In that case, we could waste days sitting here for nothing."

"I understand that."

"And if he gets spooked, then maybe knowing someone's on him will help him to make a mistake. He'll rush, get sloppy, maybe meet up with his friends, and one of them will get sloppy thinking someone's on them too."

"That's a lot of hoping," Jones said.

"Look, if we scare them into leaving, is that going to be any different than if we sit here and don't find them, then they leave in a few days, anyway?"

"Perhaps not."

"At least this way we can put some pressure on. We go on the offensive. Make them play defense instead of the other way around."

"I hear what you're saying, and I guess I agree."

"Well thanks so much, Dad. Are you gonna be able to get into her phone?"

"That depends."

"On?"

"How well she has it protected. If she has her bluetooth on, I may be able to get in that way, intercepting the signal. There's other ways too, of course, and I'll try them, see what I can do."

"How much time do you need?"

"That depends. How far away from her apartment are you?"

Recker looked at Haley, who was driving. "Twenty minutes?" Haley nodded, confirming the time. "Yeah, about twenty minutes."

"That should be enough time. Regardless, check with me first before you actually approach her."

"Will do."

"That way I can hopefully get into her phone and listen in on any calls she makes after you leave."

"I'll let you know. Good thing you used to work for a secretive company before, huh?"

"Yes, it appears my NSA training has not gone in vain. Let's just hope this works."

"It'll work," Recker said. "It'll work."

7

Recker and Haley got to Marci Johnson's apartment in twenty minutes, just like they figured, but they didn't approach right away. It wasn't one of the apartments that had its own door leading outside. There was one entrance to the three-story building. They remained in their car for another twenty minutes, just keeping an eye on the building, keeping track of anyone walking in or out.

It wasn't one of the nicest looking buildings they'd seen. It looked like a place that wasn't kept up with most of the time. The outside was dirty; they observed a few cracks in windows, and there was graffiti on the walls. It looked like a place where people went to hide out, or people who were trying to get back on their feet after a rough stretch. They weren't yet sure which category Johnson fit into at this point, but considering her ties with Webb, they assumed it was the former.

"What are we gonna do if she isn't home?" Haley asked, keeping his eyes on the front door.

"I dunno. Keep waiting, I guess. Don't really have another option, do we?"

"No, guess not."

Recker looked at the time. "It'd be nice if David got into that phone at some point, though."

"I'm sure he's working on it."

Recker was just about to reply when his phone rang. "Well, speak of the devil."

"Is that a reference to me?" Jones asked.

"Does the shoe fit?"

"It does not."

"What took you so long? Are you in?"

"Hacking into people's phones is not as easy as putting together a jigsaw puzzle, you know. It takes time, patience, effort..."

"Yeah, yeah, did you get in or not?"

"Yes."

"Good. Now we just have to make contact."

"Did you figure out your approach yet?"

"Yeah. Knock on the door and see what she knows," Recker said.

"How original."

"We don't have time for games. First, we need to make sure she's there."

"She is."

"How do you know?"

"Didn't I just tell you I got into her phone? Her

bluetooth on her phone is on, her phone pings to the location of her apartment, so a logical deduction is that she is there as well."

"What would we do without your brilliance?"

"I shudder at the thought of you being without it."

Recker smiled, then hung up. He nudged Haley on the arm. "OK, he's in. It's our time now."

Recker and Haley got out of the car and walked across the street to the apartment building. They observed several people walk in and out without any trouble going inside. The front door wasn't locked, there was no passcode, and didn't appear to have any security system. Of course, some of the people who lived there probably preferred it that way.

Once inside, they immediately found the stairs and walked up to the third floor. They went down the hallway until they reached apartment 306. Recker knocked on the door. They heard someone moving around inside.

"Guess they're not running," Haley said. "Got nowhere to go up here."

"Unless they jump out the window."

"That's leaving the hard way."

"You never know with some people."

Recker knocked on the door again, a little harder this time. They still heard movement inside. He knocked even louder now.

"All right, all right, I'm coming!" a woman's voice yelled. "Don't bang the door down!" Seconds later, the door opened. It was Marci Johnson. "Jeez, you don't gotta be so rough." She then looked Recker and Haley over. She already knew their type. They were either law enforcement, or they were enforcement of another kind. "Who are you guys? What do you want?"

"We wanna talk to you," Recker answered.

"I'm here. So talk."

"We wanna know about Mac Webb. We understand you two know each other."

Johnson curled the left side of her face and lips, already not liking the way this was going. "Who are you? Cops?"

"We're looking for him. We wanna know where he is."

"I ain't telling you guys nothing. Now get outta here!"

Johnson took a step back, and was about to close the door, but Recker moved his leg forward, preventing it from closing.

"Hey, you got no right to do that!" Johnson said. "Get outta here before I call your boss and get you in trouble."

"We're not the police."

"What? Then who are ya?"

"That's not your concern," Recker said, sounding menacing.

He wasn't sure how he was going to play it until he got there, but now that he saw and heard Johnson, she didn't seem the type to talk easily. She needed some extra convincing. Pretending to be a cop seemed like the wrong move. She'd just clam up. Now, Recker thought the best way to play it was to pretend he was the muscle man for someone. Someone who didn't play by the rules. Recker pushed the door open further and invited himself in.

Johnson threw her arms up. "Sure, just come in like you were invited."

Haley walked in, as well, closing the door behind him. He already knew how his partner was playing it. He stood in front of the door and folded his arms, a scowl on his face, looking and acting tough.

Johnson looked back at him. "What's up with Goofy here? He don't talk?"

"He talks with his fists," Recker replied.

"Oh, you guys beat up on women, do ya?"

"Not if we can help it." Recker walked closer to her. "Or if we get what we want."

"Which is what?"

"Already told you. We want Mac Webb."

"What do you want him for?"

"That's our business."

"What makes you think I know him?"

Recker pulled out his phone and quickly scrolled to the picture Jones sent him of Webb and Johnson. "This." He showed her the photo.

Johnson made a face as she looked at it. "That was two years ago, man. I haven't seen him since then."

"Oh, really?"

"Yeah, really."

"What about the rental car you gave him?"

"What? What rental?"

"He's been seen driving a rental," Recker answered. "One that you signed out for. How you wanna explain that?"

"Um, you know..." Johnson put her hand on the back of her head and looked down, trying to think of something. She had nothing, though. "Um."

"Listen, we're not here to jam you up. As a matter of fact, we don't care about you at all. Just tell us where Webb is, and we'll be gone."

"Um, well..." Johnson took another look back at Haley, who still had the same scowl on his face. "You might not believe this."

"Try us."

"Uh, I really don't know where he is."

"You just gave him a car for no reason? You don't know anything?"

"No."

Recker could see she was going to try and play it the hard way. He had to play it harder. He had a trick that he thought would work. If not, he wasn't sure what else he'd do. But he had to give it a shot. He reached into his back pocket and removed a pair of black gloves. He put the one on his right hand first, taking it slow for effect, making sure she had the idea of what he was planning.

The sudden worried look on Johnson's face indicated that it was working. "Uh, what are you doing? What's that for?"

"I don't wanna get my hands bloody."

"Your hands? Uh, for what? What would you get them bloody for?"

Recker then put the other glove on his left hand. He snapped it against his wrist once it was on tight. "Because I don't like to be lied to."

That was all Johnson needed to hear. She instantly put her hands up in front of her and started backing away. "OK, listen, I'll tell you whatever you wanna know. Just don't hurt me."

"If you start talking honestly, I might be persuaded to put these away," Recker said, looking at his gloves.

"I don't really know much. I swear."

"Tell us what you do know. And you better start talking fast."

"OK. So, I do know Mac. But I don't know where he is right now. That's the truth."

"What about the car?"

"He just showed up here last week looking for a favor."

"What favor?" Recker asked.

"The car. He wanted to know if I'd rent a car for him. That was it. That was all he wanted."

"He tell you what it was for?"

Johnson shook her head. "No. Just said I'd be doing him a favor if I rented it and let him use it for a week or two."

"And you said yes? Just like that?"

"Well, he gave me some cash for my troubles."

"How much?"

"A thousand."

"A thousand?" Recker said. "And that's everything?"

"Yeah. Said he'd bring it back to me when he was done with it."

"So he gave you a thousand dollars just to rent a car for him?"

"That's the size of it, Mac." She then laughed to herself. "Ha, that's funny. I called you Mac, and his name is..." She saw Recker wasn't laughing and got back to her serious face. "No, I guess you're not the humorous type."

"Are you guys involved?"

She let out another laugh. "Us? No. That's a funny one."

"Why?"

"Mac's got money, travels the world, and look at me. I'm stuck here in this dump just trying to get a buck any way I can."

"Well if you're so opposite, how is it that you're friends to begin with?"

"We met at some party a few years ago. That picture you showed me. It was a big one, hundreds of people there. Maybe a thousand, I dunno. Anyway, there were a lot of drugs and alcohol being thrown around, and I eventually got to talking to him. Said he might have some work for me if I wanted it."

"Which was?"

"Just running errands, things like that."

"Do you know what he does?" Recker asked.

"Nope. Never said. And honestly, I never asked. One thing you learn real quick out here, if you wanna survive, is you don't ask questions. Asking questions gets people killed. If people want something, I do it, then get out of the way. I don't wanna know nothing about nobody."

"Met anybody he does business with?"

"No. Honestly, I've only worked for him a couple of times."

"When was the last time?"

Johnson tilted her head up to think about it. "Mm, maybe six or eight months ago."

"He was here?"

"Yeah."

Recker looked at Haley. "What kind of things do you do for him?"

"Whatever he wants. Pass an envelope to someone. Rent a car for him. Deliver a package somewhere. Whatever."

"And you don't know what he does for a living? Or how often he's in town?"

"Nope. Don't know where he lives. He told me once that he travels a lot. I think he was born in England or something. But other than that, I don't know much about him."

"How about contacting him?"

Johnson shook her head again. "Doesn't work like that. I don't contact him. He contacts me when he wants something."

"And you don't tell him when the job is done or anything? No phone calls, texts, nothing?"

"Nope. Why are you guys looking for him, anyway? Mac's not a bad guy."

"Maybe we're looking to do business with him. Who else could we talk to about him?"

"Beats me. Like I said, I don't know nothing about nobody else."

"OK."

Johnson looked surprised. Recker seemed to back off a little and take her at her word. Recker took a few steps back.

"OK," Recker said again, starting to pace around.

"Wait, so you're good? We're good now?"

"For now."

"You believe me?"

Recker grinned. "Sure. Why not? Because if you're lying to us, we'll be back. And I won't be in as nice of a mood as I am now."

"I'm not lying. I promise."

Recker nodded, then started moving closer to her. He reached into his pocket and removed a card. He handed it to her.

"What's this?"

"That's my number," Recker said. "If you hear from Webb again, you call me and let me know."

Johnson looked at the card and took it. "Uh, yeah, I'll do that. I sure will."

Recker glanced at Haley and nodded toward the door. Haley opened it as Recker walked over. Before walking out, Recker took a look back at Johnson and pointed at her.

"Remember. A phone call. Or we'll be back. You hear me?"

"Yeah," Johnson replied. "I hear you."

Recker closed the door, and he and Haley walked down the hallway.

"You didn't waste any time in there," Haley said.

"Figured she wasn't the type for sweet talking."

"You can say that again. You know darn well that she ain't calling you."

"Yeah, I know."

"You played the heavy pretty good," Haley said with a laugh. "If this whole Silencer thing don't work out for you, you might have a future with Vincent."

Recker laughed along with him. "Yeah. Maybe I do, at that."

"You took a chance with that, though. What would you have done if she didn't go for it? You'd either have to back down or lean on her even harder."

"I would have looked pretty silly backing down, and we might not have gotten anything after that, but let's be thankful it didn't come to that."

"Not sure what we got now."

Split Scope

"Well if I'm right, David should be listening in on a phone call right about now."

"You think she really does have his digits?" Haley asked.

"I don't really buy that she just let this guy have a car indefinitely without knowing what's going on. They must have a way to communicate."

"I hope you're right."

"So do I."

8

Once Recker and Haley got back to the car, Recker called Jones to see if he picked up anything yet. There was no answer. He kept trying, but Jones wasn't picking up.

"Maybe he's already got a fish on the line," Haley said.

"Yeah. Let's hope so."

While they waited for word from Jones, they kept their eyes focused on the front of the building, just in case Johnson came bursting out.

Jones saw Recker's call coming in, but had his phone on silent so as not to interrupt his listening. Johnson was making a call, and Jones wanted to focus on it completely. After a few rings, someone picked up Johnson's call.

"Yeah?" Webb greeted.

"Mac, thank god I got a hold of you."

"What are you doing calling me? You know you're not supposed to hear from me for three more days."

Johnson's voice sounded rushed, like she couldn't wait to blurt things out. "I needed to warn you."

"Warn me? About what?"

"There were people just here looking for you."

"What people?"

"I don't know their names," Johnson replied.

"How many were there? What'd they look like?"

"I don't know. Just a couple of meatheads. Two of them."

"What'd they want?"

"Just said they were looking for you. They mentioned something about maybe wanting to do business with you, but I'm not sure if that was right. Might have just been looking for you for something else."

"Cops?"

"Didn't act like cops. What do you want me to do, Mac?"

"Nothing. Don't do anything. Just sit there."

"For how long?" Johnson asked.

"Until I tell ya."

"I gotta work, Mac. I can't just sit here on my ass until you tell me I can leave."

"Forget about work. Just sit tight until I tell you it's safe to move. They're probably watching your place expecting me to show up sometime. Or they'll follow you thinking you'll lead them to me."

"What do you think they want?"

"I don't know."

"One of them gave me his card with a phone number on it. You want it?"

"Yeah, sure, give it to me."

Johnson read the number off the card. "Listen, Mac, I can't just sit here while I got work. I gotta go in tomorrow or I could get fired."

"You sit tight, Marci, until I tell you that you can move. If you get fired, I'll give you your salary for the next year in one payment, OK?"

Johnson only thought about it for a second or two. "Yeah, OK, Mac, OK. I'll sit tight."

"Now don't do anything until I tell you. You stay there."

"What if these guys show up again?"

"Don't answer the door."

"Well, that's easy for you to say. You ain't gotta worry about them busting it down."

"Don't sweat it, Marci. Just play it cool and everything will be fine. As long as they think you can't get to me, you got nothing to worry about."

"Like I said, easy for you to say."

"Just do what I tell you. I swear if you don't, you'll live to regret it."

"I'm doing it, I'm doing it."

They hung up, leaving Jones to stare at his computer screen for a moment. He called Recker immediately, putting him on speaker, as he tried to pin down where Webb's location was.

"Hey," Recker said.

"Sorry I missed your calls. I was listening to Johnson's conversation with Webb."

"She called right away?"

"Not even a minute after you left."

"What'd they say?"

"Basically, Webb wants her to stay put until he tells her otherwise," Jones replied. "He's worried you might follow her if they meet."

"Smart man."

"Unfortunately. The good news doesn't stop there, though."

"What else?"

"He mentioned something about how she wasn't supposed to hear from him for three more days."

"Three days," Recker said to himself. "That must be when whatever they're planning's going down."

"Probably. She did give him your number. I assume that's one of your prepaids?"

"Yeah. Just in case something like this happened, I was hoping he might call me to see what was going on."

"He still may. We have to hope, anyway."

"What about his location? Are you able to get it?"

Jones made a noise with his mouth. "Eh, difficult to say at the moment."

"Isn't it a yes or no?"

"Well if those are the only options, then the answer's no."

"What other option is there?"

"No, but I'm working on it."

"Oh. Should I cross my fingers?"

"Cross your toes, too."

"Should I also get out my lucky rabbit's foot?"

"If you've got one," Jones said.

"How long's this gonna take?"

"Until I have an answer."

"That's not reassuring."

"It wasn't meant to be."

"You can't give me an estimation?" Recker asked.

"It takes what it takes. I'll keep working on it."

"So what are we supposed to do in the meantime? Just sit here with our hands in our pants?"

"Uh, well, if that's what you want to do."

"Webb obviously isn't coming here after that warning. And Johnson's probably not leaving, assuming we're out here."

"You're the one that pushed it," Jones said.

"Yeah, with the confident assumption that you were going to be able to pin things down."

"I am not a miracle worker."

"Could've fooled me."

"I will do my best. But if Webb was a former MI6 agent, which we know he was, he probably employs safeguards for this sort of thing. The same as you would."

"I'm hoping he gets lazy and sloppy."

Jones looked at his screen, not seeing positive results yet. "It doesn't appear that's the case so far, otherwise I'd have it already. Looks like he's using safeguards with his location."

"Great."

"I'll call you back if I have something."

Recker put his phone on the seat between his legs and sighed. Haley knew what that meant.

"Nothing, huh?"

"Nothing," Recker replied.

"Maybe we should go back in and lean on her again. She's the weak link. Webb might not make a mistake. But she might."

"Yeah, maybe. Let's give David some more time, first."

"OK. Just in case he can't come up with anything, maybe he'll be able to spoof a message from Webb? Maybe he can send something, making it seem like Webb wants her to meet him? Like a usual spot or something."

"Might work. Could be a risk too, though."

"How's that?" Haley asked.

"They might have some type of understanding that he'll never contact her unless it's time to settle up. Or they might not have a spot. If they've got one of those deals in place, any type of message from him asking her to meet somewhere might give her a red flag. Scare her into thinking it's us playing a trick."

"Yeah."

"I think for now, our best bet is still David coming up with something."

Haley nodded. "Let's hope he does."

Recker crossed his fingers and held them up for Haley to see. "Here's hoping." The two of them waiting lasted all of about thirty seconds. "The heck with this." Recker grabbed his phone again.

"What are you doing?"

"I dunno. Something. Something's better than nothing."

Haley laughed. "Not always."

"Maybe Lawson's heard something."

"I doubt it, or she would've called."

"Maybe she doesn't know about this three-day thing."

"Shot in the dark, I guess."

Recker smiled. "Even shots in the dark land somewhere. Just not always where you intend it to go." Recker dialed.

Lawson picked up immediately. "Hey. You got something?"

"Not sure. Maybe you can help out."

"I'll do what I can," Lawson whispered. "Hold on a sec. Let me step outside so I'm not within earshot of anyone." Recker gave her a minute until she was finally outside of the building. "OK, I'm good."

"Well, we have found out that Webb's still in Baltimore."

"Are the others there?"

"Don't know yet. Can't tell. He's got a woman down here doing errands for him. Name's Marci Johnson. As far as we can tell, she's just a pawn he's using. Doubt she's involved other than knowing him."

"OK?"

"We heard them talking to each other on the phone, with Webb saying she wasn't supposed to hear from him for another three days. Those were his words. Three days. Not a few, not a couple, three exactly."

"Well that sounds like it could be something," Lawson said.

"That's what we thought. You know of anything happening with that timeline? Even if it wasn't thought to involve this bunch?"

"I mean, nothing offhand. I can quietly look into it, though. I'm not sure how far I can take it, but I'll poke around a little, see if I can come up with something."

"Thanks."

"Haven't heard anything about the other three yet?"

"Not so far," Recker answered. "My gut is that they're not here. I don't have anything to base that on, though."

"Are you sure that Webb is? Just because the woman is, doesn't mean he is too."

"We've got a picture of him off a camera. He's still here. Why that is, I don't know. But he is."

"I wonder if the others are still in the same spot, too?"

"Can't say right now."

"If they are, that could mean they're working separately for some reason."

"Could be," Recker said. "Maybe they're doing four separate deals. Or maybe they're just spreading the net out wider, hoping to get into an auction with whatever they're selling."

"Unless they're buying."

"Yeah, I still don't really know what's going on. And until we come face to face with one of these clowns, we're probably not gonna know."

"OK. I'll start checking on it. You got anything else for me?"

Recker let out a laugh. "No, that's about all we got so far. Not much."

"Hey, it's something. We gotta start somewhere."

"I'm just hoping that little bit adds up soon, 'cause it sounds like we've only got three more days to figure this out."

"I know."

"Then, all bets are off."

9

Not much time had gone by when Recker's phone rang again. Before looking at it, he assumed it was Jones, or maybe even Lawson again. But it was neither. He was a little surprised to see that it was Vincent. Recker answered, curious about what he had on his mind.

"Hope you've got good news to share?"

Vincent let out a laugh. "I guess that would depend on what side of the fence you're on."

"And which side are we on?"

"The side with information."

"What kind?"

"The kind you're looking for," Vincent said. "I've got a line on one of the men you're looking for."

"You do?"

"Piers Corbyn. The gentleman who got off in Newark."

"I know him."

"Well, we have him."

Recker scrunched his eyebrows together, unsure of what he meant by that. It almost sounded like they had captured him or something. "You have him?"

"Well, not literally. But it might as well be. We've got a meeting scheduled with him later today."

Recker's eyes almost jumped out of its sockets at the revelation. "You what?"

"We've got a meeting scheduled to discuss business."

"Uh..." Recker wasn't even sure what to say at that point. He certainly wasn't ready to hear that Vincent had already lined up a meeting with the man. "Wow. I wasn't expecting that."

"You asked me to look into it, and I did. You should know I don't mess around."

"I know. But I assumed they would be a little more elusive in being found."

Vincent laughed again. "Yes, well, perhaps they are in certain circles. They are quite easily found when you know where to look. And when you have the contacts in those circles. They have buried themselves deep, but as long as you're willing to crawl into the hole with him, you can pull them up. As long as you don't mind the mud."

Recker was still thrown for a loop. "Um, what... where is he?"

"Still in Newark."

"Still in Newark. I don't know what's going on here. We've got a line on one of the other guys... Webb. He's still in Baltimore. Seems like maybe they're all staying in the same place. Wish I could figure out what they're up to."

"I can tell you what they're up to," Vincent said.

"You can?"

"As I said, I arranged a business meeting with Corbyn. You can't arrange a meeting unless you already know what's being discussed."

"So what is being discussed?"

"Drugs and weapons, mostly. Drugs more than anything. They've apparently got some major suppliers in Europe, looking to bring their stash into the US. It would be my belief that they're spread out because they're looking at specific contacts in the cities they're now staying in. Or they're putting their merchandise up for auction, hoping to get multiple people involved in order to drive up the bid."

"What kind of supply are we talking about here?" Recker asked.

"Numbers weren't initially discussed. It is my understanding we're talking millions upon millions every year. Could be as high as fifty million every year."

"Coming or going?"

"Going. Which means the returns could be quite substantial for anyone who makes the deal. We could be talking hundreds of millions of dollars a year in profit for whoever closes the deal on this end."

"And that's if it's just one," Recker said. "If they have four separate deals going on, we could be talking close to a billion dollars a year in revenue."

"Quite possibly."

"How do these guys fit in? Are they working for themselves or working for someone else?"

"That much has not been made clear to me. I don't know if they're simply middlemen, or if they have a higher position in the arrangement."

"So about this deal... are you going to do it for your own purposes, or are you trying to find out more information for me?"

Vincent snickered. "Who said it had to be an either-or proposition? I am in the business of making money, you know."

"Not much money to be made from people who are dead."

Vincent continued laughing. "Yes, that is quite a difficult task, isn't it?"

"And if I'm on their trail, you know what that outcome will be."

Vincent cleared his throat. "Yes, I'm aware of the logistics of the matter. Have no fear. I will be attending this meeting on your behalf. Unless you would like to attend as one of my bodyguards?"

"No, don't think I can make it. I'm in Baltimore right now chasing down one of the other guys."

"All the same. As I said, I will attend this meeting, and try to find out what I can for you."

"Would your interest in helping be more at my request, or because you'd like to keep whatever they're selling out of the hands of any potential competitors, also potentially weakening your organization?"

Vincent laughed again. "Mike, your cynical nature into my altruistic behavior is shocking to me."

Now Recker joined in on the laughter. "Yeah. So when is this meeting taking place?"

"In about three hours."

"OK. Well, we believe that whatever they're planning, the timeline is in three days. Whether that's the day they expect to make a sale, or that's the day they're leaving, or something else, three days was explicitly mentioned."

"That would seem to match what was inferred to me. They said they anticipated having a resolution on this quickly."

"Did you talk to Corbyn directly?"

"No," Vincent replied. "It was through a third party. Have not talked to the man, myself."

"Then how do you know that's who you're meeting?"

"I don't. Not with a hundred percent certainty. They do know of my reputation, though. That was made abundantly clear. They know I do not meet with, or make deals with those not on top of the food chain."

"Fair enough. I guess it goes without saying, but you'll let me know how it goes?"

"You will be the first person I call."

Once Recker's call concluded, he put the phone down. His partner was naturally curious.

"What was all that about?" Haley asked. Recker relayed the conversation. "Well what do you think of that?"

Recker shrugged. "Beats me."

"Maybe one of us should go up there with him. The other one can stay here."

Recker looked at the time. "Nah, not enough time. Meeting's in about three hours. Won't get there in time."

Haley stared out the window. "You know, I just got a crazy thought."

"Probably not that much different than the one I got."

"What if we just hooked Vincent up with a major score? What if he goes into this, sees there's a lot of money in it for him, and then goes into business for himself and forgets about us?"

Recker smiled. "That's pretty much what I was thinking."

"Kind of a scary thought."

Recker shrugged again. "It is what it is, I guess. I mean, if he does, would we have found him anyway, without Vincent's help?"

"Yeah, maybe not. I guess we could also look at it

like... if Vincent was planning on helping himself here, he wouldn't need to tell us beforehand."

"Maybe. You should know... Vincent doesn't always do the most logical thing. Especially if word got out, he might not want it to get back to us that he did it behind our backs."

"That way he makes it seem like he's helping, even if he's not."

"Yeah. Assuming that's the way he's leaning. And if he's leaning towards actually helping us, and not himself, then I guess we'll know that soon enough, too."

"Which way you think it's heading?" Haley asked.

"I'd like to think we've built up enough trust over the years to where we can trust he's gonna do the right thing. Like I said, though... I guess we'll find out soon enough."

10

Vincent and his entourage pulled up to the building. There were five cars in total, with Vincent's being in the middle of them. He stayed in his car until all of his men got out, making sure there was no funny business. There were some men, presumably working for Corbyn, stationed in front of the entrance of the building. They looked on as Vincent's crew got out of their vehicles. Malloy went over to Vincent's car and opened the back door, allowing his boss to get out.

"Clear so far," Malloy said.

Vincent got out of the car and took a look around. The building he was meeting Corbyn in had three floors, none of which were in active use. At one time it was an office building, but that was several years in the past. It was still in mostly good shape, though. At least the doors and windows were still in place and the roof wasn't caving in.

Vincent started walking toward the front of the building, with Malloy, and several more of his men surrounding him. Once they got near the front, one of the men stationed near the door put his hand up to stop them.

"Corbyn said for you to go up to the third floor."

Vincent slowly rotated his head and glared at the man. "Do you know who I am?"

The man was well aware of Vincent's reputation. He gulped, not exactly comfortable with the look he was receiving. The man was just some local talent that Corbyn had hired for this job. After Corbyn and his friends were gone, the man would still be there. And angering Vincent wasn't on his list of things to put on his to-do list.

"Uh, yes, I do, Mr. Vincent. It's just, uh, Corbyn said that he only wanted you to go up there. I'm just following orders, sir."

"You go tell Mr. Corbyn that I am here. You also tell him that I do not go anywhere without my security detail. So either they go up with me, or I turn around and take my business elsewhere. You tell him that."

"Uh, yes sir, yes, right away. Wait here, please."

Vincent and his crew planted themselves in front of the door while the man went inside. There were still four more of Corbyn's men stationed out there in case anything went down, not that anyone really expected trouble. It was the usual posturing of two sides, both of whom wanted the other to know they meant business if someone started anything, and to see exactly what they might be able to get away with. In Vincent's case, you couldn't get away with much. He didn't get to where he was by letting others dictate terms to him. He did the pushing.

A minute or two later, the man emerged through the door again.

"Uh, Mr. Corbyn said you could come up with your men, sir."

Vincent grinned. "Thank you. What is your name, by the way?"

"Uh, it's Joey. Joe. Joseph. Uh, sir."

"Where is Mr. Corbyn located?"

"Third floor, sir. If you go up the stairs to the third floor, make a left, you'll see a big open space where he's at. Kind of like a waiting room or something."

"And how many men does he have up there with him?"

"He has, uh, five I think." Joey looked down, giving it more thought. "Yeah, five. No, six. Yeah, there's six up there."

Vincent smiled and tapped him on the arm. "Thank you, Joey. When this is over, look me up. Maybe I'll have a position for you."

A smile emerged on Joey's face. He was surprised, but happy. Maybe more relieved than anything. "Thank you, sir. Thank you."

"Good man."

Vincent, followed by his crew, went through the

doors, immediately finding the steps to their right. As they walked up the steps, Malloy, and two others, went ahead of their boss, making sure it was safe for him. When it came to new situations, and people, that was always their method of operation. Of course, it was usually their method even when dealing with people and places that they knew. Vincent rarely led the way.

Once they reached the third floor, Malloy and the two others went through the door first. They had their hands on their guns, just in case they needed to use them quickly. There was nobody there to greet them, surprisingly enough. They took a few steps to their left and saw Corbyn sitting in an open room. He was seated behind a small round, wooden table. There were a few other metal chairs scattered throughout the space, though his men were all standing.

"I take it you're Jimmy Malloy?" Corbyn asked.

"That's right."

"There's no tricks here, you can bring your boss in."

Malloy took a brief look at everyone and nodded. He whispered into the ears of his two colleagues as he walked back to get Vincent.

"There's one missing."

Both men nodded, staying put as Malloy went back to the stairs. Malloy opened the door and saw his boss standing there against the wall, his arms in front of his body, his left hand on his right wrist.

"How does it look?" Vincent asked.

"Suspicious."

"Why?"

"That kid down there said he had six men with him. I only count five."

"Perhaps he was including Corbyn in his counts?"

"I don't think so," Malloy answered.

"And maybe he got confused or doesn't know how to add properly?"

"Maybe. In either case, we've gotta be alert."

Vincent nodded, then looked at his other men. "Everyone be on the lookout for anything that doesn't seem right."

"And if it appears things aren't going in the right direction?"

Vincent looked at Malloy. "Then you know what needs to be done. You all know the drill. Act first and be wrong, then act second and be dead."

"You wanna go with a code?"

"If I'm ready for you to make a move, I'll just tell him I think we understand each other."

Malloy nodded. "OK." He looked at the others. "Stay sharp."

With everyone clear about their responsibilities, Malloy opened the door for his boss, and Vincent walked through it. He immediately saw two of his men standing there, where Malloy left them. With Malloy right behind him, Vincent walked past the men and into the room where Corbyn was still seated. As Vincent approached, Corbyn stood up and stuck his hand out to greet the crime boss. Vincent shook his hand.

"It's a real pleasure to meet you," Corbyn said. "I've heard a lot about you."

"And you as well."

Corbyn slightly turned his head, a little surprised to hear those words. He tried as much as possible to remain in the background, not letting details slip out about him to the outside world. "You have?"

"It's my business to know things about the people I may be dealing with."

Corbyn grinned. "Yes, I'm sure." He sat down, with Vincent mimicking the position.

"So, what is it that you have to sell?"

"Right to the point, huh?"

"I'm a busy man, Mr. Corbyn. A lot of things require my attention. I don't have time to play games or make pleasantries. There's a business deal to discuss here, so let's discuss it."

"Fine. OK. I am acting in the interests of another party to facilitate a deal between them and whoever bids the highest. You're not the only one I'm talking to."

"I figured as much."

"It will be going to an auction, and everyone has to put their bids in within the next day or two, then on day three, we'll inform the person who won, make the arrangements, then we'll start the transaction."

"So we're conducting this like we're in an auction house?" Vincent asked.

"This is how the sellers prefer it. Not necessarily the way I would do it, but it's their call."

"And you get a fee for brokering the deal?"

"Yes."

"There are a lot of questions to be answered. What am I buying, the terms of the deal, how the merchandise will be transported, all of that."

Corbyn looked over at one of his men and motioned at him with one finger. The man grabbed a silver briefcase and came over to the table, setting the briefcase down. Corbyn unlocked it, opened it, then turned it around so his guest could take a look. Vincent looked at the bags of white powder that filled the briefcase. He reached in and took one out, analyzing it.

"Pure heroin," Corbyn said.

Vincent laughed. "Pure... yes, well, that's a word that gets thrown around a lot, hoping to take advantage of some suckers eager for a fix. It's usually mixed with other substances then marketed as pure."

"It's the real deal."

"I guess I only have your word to take for that, don't I? And what is the price tag?"

Corbyn threw his hands up. "That's for you to determine. Just between you and me, I expect the winning bid to be around forty or fifty million."

"That's a lot of money."

"It's a lot of heroin. You'll be able to make that back in no time. As a matter of fact, you might spend fifty million, but you'll make three times that much, easy."

"In this line of business, nothing is easy."

"I guess that's why you're the top dog, though, isn't it?"

"And the delivery?"

"One shipment. Two months from now."

"From where?" Vincent asked.

Corbyn shrugged. "I don't know. I think the original spot is Pakistan, then to Europe, then will be delivered to here. Once it's off the ship, you load it into your trucks, take it wherever you want, then distribute it from there."

"And in terms of the money?"

"Five million deposit up front to the winning bidder. Then half gets put down next month, then the other half gets paid upon delivery of the product."

Vincent put the bag back into the briefcase. He leaned back in his chair and put his hand on his chin, staring at the briefcase, thinking about the proposition.

"That's a lot of money upfront."

"It's a business deal," Corbyn said. "Nobody's trying to swindle anyone. If this goes through without problems, it could lead to a long-term relationship. This won't be their only shipment, mate. This is a heavy operation."

"I don't know. I prefer doing business with people I know."

"You know me."

"But I don't know who you're working for," Vincent said. "Unless you'd care to divulge the names?"

Corbyn smiled. "Can't do that."

"What about the others?"

"What others?"

"Your partners."

"I ain't got no partners. Just doing this deal like I said. Just me."

Vincent put his hand up and snapped his fingers. "Jimmy, what were their names again?"

Malloy immediately answered. "Logan Harris. Mac Webb. And Rory Zouch."

"Yes, those were the ones."

Corbyn sat there, motionless, not any type of expression on his face. He stared at Malloy for a few moments, then let his eyes return to Vincent. "So I got partners, so what?"

"It matters a great deal to me, Mr. Corbyn, that I know exactly who I'm dealing with in all business dealings."

"OK, so you know our names. So?"

"Perhaps you'd like to explain why you're in four different cities?"

"What makes you think we're in four different cities?"

Vincent leaned forward. "You're in my territory. You may be a big deal in your own country, but you're in mine now. Nothing goes on here, on a deal of this magnitude, that I don't know about."

Split Scope

"Again, don't see the problem. We're trying to spread ourselves out, talk to as many people as we can, trying to line up the best possible deal. So what?"

"The problem is, on a deal such as this, if you were to make a deal with someone else, one of my competitors, or someone on a lower footing as me, it might give them enough money to possibly challenge me, or take me on, or hope to gain more power in this region. And I'm afraid I can't have that."

"Look, all we're trying to do is make the best deal. If it's with you, then you don't gotta worry about any of that other stuff, do you?"

"So how does a bunch of ex-MI6 agents wind up being brokers for major drug operations?"

Corbyn stared at him again. It seemed as if Vincent had more information on him than he cared for. "What makes you think we're ex-MI6?"

"As I said, do you really think I don't know exactly who I'm dealing with? I make it a point to know everything."

"Perhaps too much."

"No such thing as knowing too much."

"I beg to differ." Corbyn then reached across the table and shut the briefcase. He slid it back to him and locked it again. "I think maybe I'll do my business elsewhere."

Vincent put his hand out to try and diffuse any rising tension. "Don't be so hasty. I'll try to help you."

Corbyn stood up. "Try and help me? What are you

talking about? If you ain't buying, you've got nothing I want."

"Well you're wrong again right there. I can offer you a lot more than money right now."

"And what's that?"

"Your life. I would assume that's worth more, but then again, some people don't seem to value theirs that much."

"I still don't know what you're talking about. Sounds like a lot of malarkey."

Vincent put his hands out toward the chair, hoping Corbyn would sit back down. He did.

"There are people looking for you," Vincent said. "Very powerful, and dangerous people."

"Like who?"

"That I can't divulge. But they're looking, and they're coming. And when they find you, you won't be able to get your money from this deal. Because you'll be dead."

"Sounds like more talk. If you're talking about your government, or even mine for that matter, it's not happening. MI6, CIA, Mossad, KGB, and any other organization you can think of, I know how to disappear. They won't find me. I've got more aliases, and passports, and friends in low places than you can shake a stick at."

"Everybody can be found. It's just a matter of when. Not if."

"Even if that's true, what's it got to do with me? What do you want?"

"Give me the locations of your partners, and perhaps I can persuade those people to let you escape unharmed."

Corbyn looked at him like he was crazy. "Are you out of your mind? Turn on my partners? Won't happen."

"I would beg you to think differently."

"Why? What's it to you?"

"Me? Nothing. I just figure this way might be faster."

"Who exactly are we talking about that's coming? And who do they work for? CIA? FBI?"

"Who doesn't matter. But they're probably more dangerous than you are. And to my knowledge, this is not an official government matter."

"If it's not government, then what do they want us for? What'd we do to them?"

"To my knowledge, you killed a friend of theirs when your allegiances were maybe not quite as clear as they are now."

Corbyn's face seemed to indicate a clearer understanding of the situation now. "Ah, so it is a government job."

Vincent shook his head. "I don't think so. If it was really the government after you, you probably wouldn't even be here right now. No, this is someone who might have ties to the government, who knows what you did, and now they want payback. They want retribution. And believe me, they won't stop until they get it."

"You really think I'm going to start running scared because of some ghost out there? They should be afraid of me. Of us."

Vincent grinned. "Well, I'm certainly glad I'm not in your position. Because if I was, I probably wouldn't be sleeping nights."

"I think we're done here."

"Before you go, I would ask you to carefully reconsider my offer. Your life for the locations of your friends."

"That's just stupid talk, mate. I won't do it. I'll take my chances with this ghost-like figure you're afraid of."

"I'm not afraid, but then again, he's not after me. I strongly urge you to reconsider. Whatever deal you think you can line up, you'll never make it. You won't see a dime."

"Like I said, I'll take my chances." Corbyn stood up again. "We're done here."

11

Corbyn walked past Vincent, and motioned for his men to follow him. Malloy, though, stood in his way. And he wasn't moving. Malloy and Corbyn stood face-to-face, looking like they were about to throw down with each other at any moment.

"Vincent isn't done talking to you," Malloy said.

"Well I'm done talking to him. And if you don't move, you'll be eating through a straw for the next year."

Malloy grinned. "I don't think so."

"Gentlemen, gentlemen," Vincent said. He turned around, but didn't get out of his seat. "Let's have cooler heads prevail here. Mr. Corbyn, would you please return to your seat?"

Corbyn finally took his eyes off Malloy and looked at Vincent. "Why?"

"Because our business has not concluded."

"I think it has. You're doing nothing here but wasting my time."

"I beg to differ." Vincent put his hand out toward the seat Corbyn was previously sitting in. "Please."

Corbyn sighed, and took a step back from Malloy as he contemplated the offer. After a few seconds, he finally decided to return to the table. He wasn't sure why. Maybe he had hopes that Vincent might change his mind. Maybe the crime boss was playing hardball with him, and when he saw that Corbyn wasn't budging, decided to try a different tactic. Maybe he'd relent. Little did Corbyn know, relenting wasn't in Vincent's vocabulary, either.

"So, you have an offer or not?"

Vincent smiled. "Yes, I have an offer. My offer is for you to tell me where your friends are, and I will guarantee your survival. At least until you get back to your own country, or wherever it is that you want to go. After that there's nothing I can do."

Corbyn immediately scoffed. "That's not an offer. I already told you, I'm not afraid of whoever this mystery guy or group is. I don't care about them. I can handle myself."

Vincent nodded. "Yes, I'm sure you can."

"Why do you care so much, anyway? What's in it for you?"

Vincent shrugged. "Nothing, I suppose. One, I'm not really interested in your deal or what you're selling. Two, by getting rid of you people, keeps the product and the money out of the hands of competitors and people who may eventually rise to challenge me, making the path more difficult. And three, I made a promise to someone that I'd look into it. And I am a man of my word. That means you and your people are on borrowed time."

"This is ludicrous. I don't have to sit here and listen to it any longer."

As Vincent and Corbyn continued talking, getting a little more heated, Malloy started moving around the room. With most eyes on the two men at the table, Malloy used the opportunity to slide in behind Corbyn's men, eventually making his way over to the window, where one of the men was standing.

"That's my final offer," Vincent said. "I hope you'll consider it."

"Well, I think we both know what you can do with that offer, don't we?" Corbyn replied.

"It looks like we understand each other."

That was the only cue Malloy needed. He immediately grabbed the unsuspecting man next to him, and violently threw him through the window. The man was so surprised at the action, he didn't even have a chance to fight back. Glass shattered everywhere, as the man fell three stories to his death on the ground below, the back of his head smacking against the concrete.

As soon as he tossed the man through the window, Malloy didn't bother to look at the damage outside, as he immediately pulled out his gun and pointed it at one of the other men. The rest of Vincent's men did the same. Corbyn's men instantly looked around, seeing all the guns pointed at them, not having a chance to pull theirs.

Corbyn looked stunned as he looked around the room. "What the hell is this?" He stared at Malloy. "You threw a guy out the bloody window."

"Sure did," Malloy replied.

"What the hell is wrong with you people? I come here in good faith, hoping to make a deal with you." He then looked at Vincent. "I was told you were a man of principle."

"I'm a man of my word," Vincent said. "Unfortunately, I gave that word to someone else first."

"This is ridiculous. What do you hope to gain by this?"

"I hope to gain the exact locations of your partners."

"Won't happen. I'm not gonna tell you."

Malloy took aim at another of Corbyn's men, and instantly pulled the trigger without another thought. He dropped to the ground... dead.

"It looks as though the numbers of your men are rapidly declining," Vincent said.

"So? I barely even know these guys. I hired them for a few jobs. Kill all of them for all I care."

Vincent looked at Malloy and shrugged. Malloy then looked at the rest of his men and nodded. Almost

Split Scope

immediately, they opened fire on the remaining members of Corbyn's crew.

Corby's eyes were wide open. "I didn't think you'd actually do it!"

"I am not someone who messes around," Vincent said. "I'll do what I say I'll do. Now, the locations of your partners?"

Before Corbyn was able to say anything, another shot rang out. This time, it wasn't from the hand of one of Vincent's men. Vincent jumped in his chair and swiftly turned his head toward where the shot came from. Malloy's eyes darted all around, trying to locate where the shooter was. One of Vincent's men fell to the ground.

"That sixth guy," Malloy said.

"You know what to do," Vincent said, motioning with his hand.

Malloy pointed down the hall. "Get him."

The rest of Vincent's men took off to get the last shooter. Only Malloy stayed behind. He kept a gun pointed right at Corbyn.

"Now, where were we?" Vincent asked.

"You were just about to let me go," Corbyn answered.

Vincent laughed. "Oh yes. The locations?"

"That's right. You can go fly a kite."

"Mr. Corbyn. Surely you realize by now that you're not just going to waltz out of here until you give me the information that I'm asking for."

"And surely by now you realize that I'm not giving you nothing. And you're right, I was MI6, so if you think you're going to be able to just sit here for ten or twenty hours torturing me, you can just forget it. I can resist any torture method you got. It don't scare me."

"I was hoping we'd be able to come to some sort of understanding. Like two intelligent businesspeople."

"I don't think so."

Corbyn jumped up out of his chair, reaching for the gun he had inside his jacket. But he was an easy target for Malloy, who still had his gun aimed at him. Malloy fired three times, and at that range, he couldn't miss. And at that range, it was easily fatal. Corbyn failed to get a shot off, or even aim the gun properly, with the weapon falling out of his hand upon the impact of the bullets, his body falling backwards over the chair.

Vincent remained seated, in the same position he was in, hardly moving an inch. It was almost as if there were no confrontation at all. His face was stoic. Finally, he moved his head to the side, looking around the table at Corbyn's lifeless body. One of Corbyn's legs was still propped up on top of the chair.

"It seems as if Mr. Corbyn has rejected our deal." Vincent's voice was calm.

Malloy went over to the window and looked down, seeing the dead body on the ground. He also saw the guards stationed out front, just looking up at him, wondering what exactly was going on.

Malloy yelled down to them. "You guys wanna make an issue out of it?"

Joey looked at the others and yelled back. "No."

Malloy looked back at his boss. "What do you wanna do about these guys out here?"

Before Vincent was able to reply, they heard several more shots, coming from the other end of the floor. They assumed that was the sixth man that was hiding. They looked in that direction, waiting for the rest of their men to return. They did, letting Vincent know the last man had been eliminated.

"Dude's a goner," one of the men said.

"Excellent," Vincent said.

"What about these guys?" Malloy asked.

"Go down, tell them I'd like to speak with them. I'll be right out."

As Malloy left, he took another guard with him, and told a couple of the others to stay back with Vincent. If there was going to be any shooting out there, he didn't want the boss to be involved. Just a few minutes later, one of Vincent's men came back up.

"Jimmy says it's safe to come down."

Vincent looked at him and nodded, then proceeded to go back down to the first floor. With guards in front of him, Vincent walked outside, seeing Joey and his partners standing next to Malloy.

"Any of you got a problem with what went on up there?" Vincent asked.

Joey and the others looked at each other, then

shook their heads. "We don't even know what happened," Joey said.

"Good. Keep it that way. Any of you upset, or angry, about what happened? Feel like you need to avenge something?"

"Mr. Vincent, I'm sure whatever happened up there was, well... I guess what I'm trying to say is... we're not friends with Corbyn or part of his group or anything. We were just hired to stand out here. Stand guard."

Vincent closely looked the three of them over. They looked the part of people he might have some use for. "You guys together?"

"Uh, we all know each other, yeah."

"How much were you getting paid for this?"

"Like, fifty bucks each. We didn't exactly get our money yet, though. Guess we're not getting it now."

Vincent turned around and put his hand on the shoulder of one of his men, whispering in his ear. "Grab the stash out of the car."

The man instantly left. He came back a minute later, holding a white envelope, which he promptly gave to Vincent. Vincent looked inside and pulled out some money.

"Here, hold your hands out," Vincent said, sticking a few bills into each of their hands. "Here's two hundred for each of you."

"Wow, thanks Mr. Vincent," Joey replied. "That's really good of you. Thank you."

Vincent handed the envelope back to his man, and looked the three men over again. "You boys working?"

"Nothing steady, sir."

Vincent nodded. "Well, if you're looking for some steady income, and want a job, maybe we can work something out."

"That'd be great, sir. We'd really appreciate that."

"You boys trustworthy?"

"You can count on us for anything, sir. We won't let you down."

"I hope not. 'Cause if you do, you might wind up like those guys upstairs."

"Not us, sir."

"OK. Get back to me in a few days if you're still interested."

Vincent turned and left, walking back to his car. Several of his other men left with him, surrounding him on the way there. Malloy stayed behind. He tapped Joey on the shoulder, and handed him a business card. After Joey took it, Malloy tapped him playfully on the cheek and smiled.

"Good boy." Malloy went back to the car, getting in the back seat next to his boss. "Went down pretty much like you thought it would."

"Yes," Vincent replied. The car started moving. "Almost exactly."

"Think Recker will be mad we took him out already? We didn't get anything out of the guy first."

"No, I think Mike will be fine with the result. I believe he has the same intention."

"It's a lot of money we're passing up here. Could be a sweet deal for us."

Vincent nodded as he thought about it. "Yes, it could have been."

"We could still take out the rest and accept the deal at the same time. Maybe leave one remaining."

Vincent rubbed around his mouth. "No, I don't think that would work. I value our relationship with Recker more than I do a few million dollars."

"With all due respect, and I like Recker as much as anyone, it's a little more than a few million dollars. I mean, we're talking a hundred million, if not more."

"We have plenty of money," Vincent said. "We don't even know what to do with all the money we have now. No, money is not the be-all-end-all. You get to where we are by building relationships. People you know you can trust. People you know you can turn your back on without getting a knife in it. People you know you can believe in."

"Yeah, I suppose you're right."

"We're in the Recker-business. And I think that's a pretty good place to be."

12

Recker's phone rang. It was a nice sound to hear after the past few hours of sitting there in silence, other than hearing Haley's voice, along with his own.

Upon seeing it was Vincent calling, Recker wondered if things were about to get more interesting. "Maybe business is about to pick up." He answered the phone. "Yeah?"

"Mike," Vincent greeted. "How are things at your end?"

"Uh, pretty slow, I guess. How 'bout yours?"

"Well, that is what I'm calling about. It looks like the man in Newark will no longer be a problem for you. You don't have to search for him anymore."

Recker had an idea of where this was going, but let Vincent explain. "Why's that?"

"It appears he met with an unfortunate accident."

"He's dead?"

"That would be correct."

"What happened?"

"As I told you, I had a meeting with him. It did not go as well as I had hoped."

"As well for who?"

"For anyone," Vincent answered. "I tried to get some information out of him, but he was a pretty stubborn guy. One of those go down with the ship type of people."

"I understand."

"I assumed you wouldn't be too broken up about it, considering it's what you were likely to do, anyway."

"Yeah, I'm not upset. Just wish we could've gotten something out of him first."

"All is not lost on that front."

"What do you mean?" Recker asked.

"I know why they're here."

"You do?"

"He explained it to me very succinctly."

"What are they doing here?"

"They're acting as agents for another party. I believe they said the person they were working for was in Pakistan."

"Nice. What's their play?"

"Drugs. Heroin, to be precise. And a lot of it. Price tag of around fifty million."

Recker whistled. "That's a pretty big price tag."

Split Scope

"In his estimations, we could've doubled or tripled our money on it."

"That's a big score."

"It is. From what I gather, the four men were in different cities, trying to get bids in. They were, or are, doing some type of auction. Sealed bids."

"That's interesting. So it's just drugs they're peddling?"

"As far as I know. Maybe there's something else, but that's all he told me. The shipment would come in around two months from now. Down payment now, the other half in a month, then the rest upon delivery."

"All coming in at one time?"

"That seemed to be the suggestion," Vincent replied.

"They're working for someone else?"

"That was the implication."

"Any chance they're really working for themselves, and just pretending they're in the middle?"

"There's always a chance. Whether that's the case, I didn't get to talk to him long enough to find out more. Like I said, he was a stubborn guy. Didn't seem to value his own health much. Too busy worrying about betraying his partners."

"Wonder if the others are going to be the same? If they're a tight-knit group, might be helpful once we find the others. If they're close, they won't give up their partners."

"If they're like Mr. Corbyn, I think it is unlikely."

"Well, thanks for the assist," Recker said.

"I can continue digging around for the others, if you like. I don't think I'll be able to get close to them again, though."

"Why not?"

"If the man informed his partners that he was meeting with me, then he suddenly shows up dead, it doesn't take a genius to put two and two together. I'm pretty sure none of them would be willing to take that chance with me."

"Yeah, I see what you mean."

"Nonetheless, I can still dig around, put my network of contacts to work. Maybe they can help dig up something."

"Well, at least that's something. I appreciate the help."

"No problem."

"Was it tough?" Recker asked. "Walking away from that kind of deal?"

Vincent laughed. "Not as much as some people might think. I'm a man of my word, Mike. Always have been. Always will be. You and I have an understanding with each other. No amount of money is worth breaking that."

"Even when those bags are stuffed with cash and overflowing?"

Vincent laughed again. "Not even if the boat the stuff was coming in on was made of gold. Sometimes you reach a point in life when you already have all the money you need. Getting more of it doesn't really interest you anymore. It's just about maintaining what you have. I think that's where I am now."

"Good perspective to have. I appreciate it."

"If I come up with anything else, I'll let you know."

Once he hung up, Recker let his partner know of Corbyn's demise.

"Well, I guess it's good to know Vincent's still on our side," Haley said.

Recker took a deep breath. "One down, three to go."

"I don't mind Corbyn getting eliminated, but it's not really gonna help our case any."

"How's that?"

"As soon as the others hear about it, they'll clam up good and tight. They're not gonna take any chances now."

"Maybe. But if they just think it's an isolated incident, or a fluke or something, they might still be vulnerable."

"You know as well as I do they're not gonna think that," Haley said. "These guys are pros. If this was me and you, and one of our partners got killed, you know darn well you're not gonna keep operating like it's business as usual. You're gonna circle the wagons first, figure out what went wrong, not take any risks."

"In a normal situation, yeah. But we already know these guys are on a schedule. They might not have time to sit and wait."

"Yeah, that's true."

"We gotta hope that works in our favor." Recker scoffed at his own suggestion. "Of course, that assumes we can even get close to any of them, anyway."

Recker grabbed his phone and started dialing.

"Who are you calling?" Haley asked.

"Lawson. Should let her know one of them's down. Should also..." His words were interrupted by the sound of Lawson's voice.

"Hey, you got something?"

"Just wanted to let you know one of them's dead."

"Which one?"

"Corbyn."

"How'd it happen?"

"Don't exactly know," Recker replied. "Wasn't us."

"Then who was it?"

"Just someone we got working on it with us."

"OK. Thanks for letting me know. How are we on the others?"

"Still working on it."

"Doesn't sound promising."

"Well, one out of four isn't bad. In addition, we found out what they're doing here."

"Well that's something. I've been trying to poke my nose into things around here, but I keep getting stonewalled."

"It's a big drug shipment," Recker said. "I think they're the go-between guys. Probably setting it up and arranging everything for a hefty fee."

"What kind of drugs?"

"Heroin. Word I got is the price tag's about fifty million. Street value could be double or triple that."

"That's a major deal."

"Yeah."

"I wonder if that's why I was told to stay back," Lawson said. "Maybe they're wanting this deal to go through so they can try to find out who the person or group is behind it."

"Could be. Think the deal might be originating out of Pakistan."

"Probably not shipping from there. Probably shipping from Europe."

"Most likely. I was told that we're probably looking at two months from now for shipment. Half down next month."

"That would make sense. Once they get payment, it might take twenty or thirty days for the boat to arrive. Which would mean it's close to being ready, if it's not already."

"I'd say it's likely that the agency is hoping that these guys will lead to whoever this supplier is," Recker said.

Lawson sighed loudly into the phone, considering her options. "Be nice if they told me something."

"What do you want us to do? Keep on it or pull back?"

"No, don't pull back. Because if we're wrong about

this, then we might let them go for nothing. And I can't let that happen."

"If we go further on this and ruin a major CIA operation, it won't look good on you if it comes back to you."

"I shouldn't have been shut out on this to begin with. But if it does come back to me, I'll deal with it. I've built up enough goodwill over the years that even if it does, the fallout shouldn't be too bad."

Recker snickered. "I should be prime example number one that goodwill doesn't buy you much."

"You were a special case. Still are. That wasn't the norm."

"OK, well, that's your business. If you want us to keep after them, then we will."

"I do."

"I'm not sure if there's much I can do to help you on the street level, but maybe I can work backwards, figure out the angle from Pakistan and work from there."

"Whatever works for you."

Recker hung up and put the phone down in the cupholder between the seats. He let out a sigh and shook his head as he looked out the windshield.

"What are you thinking?" Haley asked.

"I'm thinking this thing's going completely off the rails."

"How so?"

"I dunno. Just seems we're going in different directions without having a clear understanding of what's going on."

"Well, we knew that when we started."

"Yeah. Just hoped it would get better." Recker grabbed his phone again. "David's gotta have something. We can't just sit here. If not, we gotta make a move and force something to happen." He dialed Jones' number, who picked up on the third ring.

"Yes?"

"Where are you on this?"

"Same place as I was before," Jones answered.

"That wasn't what I wanted to hear."

"Didn't think it would be. But it's where I'm at."

"Why can't you find anything?"

"Because Webb is a former secret agent who seems to excel in not wanting to be found?"

"Well aren't you supposed to be a former NSA agent that excels in finding people and things that don't want to be found?"

"Really, Michael?"

"Just saying."

"There's not much I can do against people who take extreme precautions in guarding their privacy."

"What's this guy doing that's so special that even the great David Jones can't find him?"

"I'll say this in terms even a child can understand," Jones said. "The signal that Johnson used to call him is bouncing in so many different directions it's making my head spin. I cannot pin it down to a single location."

"Can you eliminate any of them?"

"Sure, I can eliminate the ones that are coming out of Florida, or Colorado, or Spain, or a dozen other ones. But that doesn't erase the dozens of ones that are coming up in Baltimore." Recker loudly sighed. "I know you're frustrated, but I'm doing what I can do."

"We're running out of time."

"I'm painfully aware of that."

"I don't think we can keep waiting."

"Which means what?" Jones asked. "What other options do you have?"

"I think it's time to go to Plan B."

"Which is?"

"Time to amp up the pressure."

"I'm not sure I like the sound of that."

Recker smirked. "They won't either."

13

With Jones on speaker, and Haley sitting next to him, Recker started going over his plan. He wasn't sure it would work, but he wasn't sure it wouldn't either. Even if it didn't, it was better than just sitting there for another day or two.

"So exactly what is this grand plan of yours?" Jones asked.

"Didn't say it was grand," Recker replied. "I just said it's time to ramp up the pressure."

"And you think you have the solution?"

"Nope. Just think I have a solution. Not *the* solution. Could fail spectacularly."

"Well that doesn't sound encouraging. It already sounds like we're getting off on the wrong foot."

"You haven't heard it yet."

"I don't have to. You've already made it sound terrible."

"Can I say it now?"

"Since when did you ever need my permission to talk about one of your plans?"

"So we've already got Webb's number, right?" Recker said.

"Yeah."

"So let's give him a call."

Jones seemed stunned. "What?"

"We have his number. We can't find him. Let's call him and see if he wants to meet."

Haley didn't really have an opinion yet. Not until he heard more of the plan. Jones, though, didn't have good vibes about it.

"That's the plan?" Jones asked. "That's terrible."

"Why?" Recker replied.

"Because there's no way that Webb is going to meet you."

"How do you know?"

"First of all, that number we have of him from Johnson probably isn't his real number. For all we know, that might be the only number he uses just for her. No one else might have it. Second, if you call him, he'll know right away something's fishy. There is no way he'll respond to you in a positive way. There's nothing you can say to change that."

"Nothing?"

"That's what I said."

"I'll frame it in a way that suggests I wanna do business," Recker said.

"He'll never buy that. Not now."

"Won't know unless we try."

"I don't see any way in which this will work."

"Look, maybe it's a long shot, and maybe it has no chance of working, but where else are we right now?"

"I say let's do it," Haley said. "If we can't find him any other way, each hour that goes by is time he's using to get farther away from us."

"He'll know it's a trap the moment you talk to him," Jones said.

"Could be. But it also might be that he thinks we're getting closer to him and slips up somewhere."

"I can't believe that. Not with this bunch. They're not some run-of-the-mill thugs that just came in from the street corner. These are highly trained professionals."

"Even professionals make mistakes sometimes," Recker said. "Especially if they think someone's after them."

"And what do you think will happen? He's going to just magically agree to a meeting with no questions asked?"

"My thinking is that if it's a number that only Johnson has, and now we have it, he's going to think she talked and gave up whatever she knows about him."

"Which might be next to nothing."

"Possibly," Recker said. "But there are a few other

options, too. If she knows more, he might try to come here and silence her."

"He'll assume you're watching. He won't do that."

"Probably not. Or he could try and lure her somewhere and try the same thing, seeing if someone's following her."

"You're putting the woman's life in danger?"

"She put her own life in danger," Recker answered. "We're not responsible for that. She chose to work with these people."

"And if none of those things happen?"

"Then maybe Webb gets skittish and takes off somewhere, and we can pick him up somehow."

"That is a long shot."

"Didn't say it wasn't. But it's better than just sitting and waiting."

"But sitting and waiting might lead us to a better position," Jones said.

"I'm with Mike," Haley said. "Let's turn up the heat."

"Of course you're with Mike. Why do you two always think alike?"

"Probably because we have the same background," Recker replied. "Look, it doesn't look like we're gonna take him by surprise. So we gotta do the next best thing."

"Let him know we're coming?" Jones asked.

"He already knows we're coming. Johnson's already told him about us. But he doesn't know who we are.

For all he knows, we're just a couple guys looking to get in on the action."

"I still think it's doomed to failure."

"Could be."

"And what if you contact him, and he moves up his timeline? And he's gone tomorrow? What then? We've lost him."

"We're losing them by sitting here," Recker said. "At least if we do this, something's happening. We put the wheels in motion. We're putting the chess pieces on the board. Right now, the board's not even on the table."

"I love your analogies."

"Does it work?"

"I don't know. You're going to do it anyway, aren't you?"

"Yeah."

"Then what are you asking me for?"

"Just wanted you to be on board."

"And if I'm not?"

"Then I'm gonna do it, anyway."

Jones laughed. "Then what was all this about?"

"Well, maybe you'd come up with something insightful to make me change my mind. But you didn't."

"Sorry to disappoint you."

"Not the first time," Recker sarcastically said.

"Someone who didn't know you better might be offended."

Recker chuckled. "Probably."

"What if this guy doesn't respond when you call?"

"I don't know. I hadn't considered it."

"You hadn't considered it? Ha, this should be interesting."

"I'll give it a try now. I'll let you know how it goes."

"I'm sure you will."

Before calling Webb, Recker looked over at his partner.

"What are you gonna say?" Haley asked.

Recker shrugged. "That we're looking to buy, I guess."

"He's gonna ask you how latched on to Johnson."

Recker sighed. "Yeah."

"Need to figure out something good. If he doesn't buy it, it's game over right there."

Recker thought for a minute, not really coming up with much. The only thing he could think of was blaming it on Johnson. "What if I just say she let it slip out somewhere? She mentioned it to the wrong people, word got back to me, and here we are."

"I'm not sure that'll do it."

"I'll have to make him believe it."

"Might be a tough sell."

"Like I said, I'll have to make him believe it."

Recker dialed the number they had for Webb. It kept ringing over and over with no answer. He looked over at his partner and shook his head.

"Possibility also exists that he ditched the phone the moment Johnson told him about us," Haley said.

Recker raised his eyebrows and tilted his head, knowing that was a real possibility. All he could do was hope that wasn't the case and that, at some point, Webb would pick up. Recker kept trying. Three separate times, he called, though he wasn't successful in getting through on any of them.

Recker put his phone back down. "I'll try again in a few minutes. Maybe he doesn't carry that phone with him."

"Maybe we should go in and have another round with Johnson. She might know more than she told us."

"Probably does."

"She might have an alternative way to contact him, too."

"Let's wait a few more minutes, then try this again. If it still doesn't work, we'll try Johnson again."

Recker waited twenty more minutes, wanting to give Webb some time to finish whatever he was doing and get to the phone. That was assuming Webb still had it, of course. He picked up the phone and dialed the number again. He was pleasantly surprised when someone actually answered this time.

"Who's this?" It was an American accent, so Recker knew it wasn't Webb, unless he was good at disguising his voice, which couldn't be ruled out.

"I'm looking for Webb," Recker said.

"And just who are you?"

"The name's John Smith."

"Well that sounds totally legitimate."

"Maybe it is, maybe it's not," Recker said. "I'm still looking for Webb."

"Don't know who that is."

Recker laughed. "Come on, man, this is his phone that you're answering. Of course you know him. Let's not play games here, huh? My time's valuable, and I'm sure yours is too. So let's just cut to the chase and get Webb for me, huh?"

"What do you want him for?"

"I'm looking to make a deal. What do you think I want him for?"

"Could be a lot of reasons."

"No, I'm a cop looking to lock him up. I just figured I'd call him first to let him know I'm coming. I mean, come on."

"What is it that you think he's got?"

"I've been hearing he's looking to sell something," Recker answered.

"Such as?"

"I've heard he's got some merchandise he'd like to get rid of. Say, fifty million worth of merchandise?"

"How you know about this?"

"I told you. I've heard things. I can't go revealing my sources, but if the information's legit, we might be able to talk some business."

"You able to come up with that?"

"Depends on the terms. That's why I wanna talk to Webb."

"Maybe he ain't here."

"Then maybe you need to get him," Recker replied. "My offer isn't good for eternity, and if he can't supply what I need, there are other people I can go to."

"All right. I'll let him know you called. Where can he reach you if he's interested?"

"Right here. Tell him to make it soon. If I don't have a call within the hour, I'll go elsewhere."

Once Recker hung up, he looked at his partner and gave a shrug.

"Seemed to go OK so far," Haley said.

"Yeah. Now we'll see if I actually get a call back."

"What do you think the chances are?"

"I dunno. Fifty-fifty?"

"Guess that's as good as we can hope for right now."

They patiently waited for thirty minutes. Or at least as patiently as they could. Recker did a lot of finger tapping as he waited for that call.

"They could be trying to run a make on you," Haley said.

"Can't do a whole lot with John Smith."

"Might be the phone number they're checking."

"That won't do them much good either."

"Well we know that, but they might be trying, anyway."

Recker didn't have a chance to respond, as his

phone started ringing. He looked at it, hoping it was Webb's number. It was. He eagerly answered it.

"Yes?"

"I hear you're looking for me," a British voice answered.

"Depends on who you are." Recker was hoping the man would say his own name.

"If you don't know, you shouldn't be calling. And speaking of calling, how'd you get this number, anyway? It's not freely handed out."

"Your friend Marci's got some loose lips. You should probably do something about that."

"Oh, I will. She just happened to give you this number?"

"Nothing just happens in this business," Recker said. "I told her I was looking to do business with you."

"And she just gave you my number? Just like that?"

"Well, there might have been some bargaining going on, and maybe a few bills being passed, but... something like that."

"I don't believe you. Marci wouldn't just give you my number."

"Why? Think you've got her trained better than that?"

"Yeah, maybe."

"Listen, we all know in this business, or any business, money talks. And if you've got enough, you can get what you want."

"And what is it that you want?"

"I hear you're looking to sell something. I'm looking to buy."

"Might be. What's your name?"

"Already told the other guy. John Smith."

"You expect me to work with that?"

"If you're looking to do business, you will."

"I need more."

"All you need is the money I'm willing to give you," Recker said. "Nothing else is important. Names, addresses, plans, none of that. You've got product, I've got money, it's as simple as that."

"Nothing's as simple as that in this game, friend. You should know that."

"Look, if you have something to sell, I'm interested. But I'm not giving you anything other than money. It behooves me and my organization to keep this as low-key as possible, otherwise there may be some people who try to prevent this transaction from happening. I obviously can't have that. If those terms don't work for you, that's fine. But those are my conditions. You can take them or leave them."

"How do I know you're on the up-and-up?"

"A suitcase full of money should do it, don't you think?" Recker asked.

"We need to have some type of meeting first."

"Fine. I guess that could be arranged."

"Before we get to that, just know that if you wanna keep everything a secret, it's gonna cost you more.

That's the price of business. If we don't know who we're dealing with, the price goes up."

"I'm OK with that. As a matter of fact, I understand this is some type of bidding auction. Is that correct?"

"That's the general terms."

"I'd like to bypass that, if possible."

"What, you think you're special? You get preferential treatment?"

"Yes," Recker replied. "Let's just end the charade and I'll bid more than you're likely to get from anyone else."

"Is that so? How much more you talking?"

"The prevailing opinion is this shipment will sell for between forty and fifty million, right?"

"Yeah, around there, I guess."

"I'll pay sixty if you just sell it to me and forget everyone else."

"So you want to rig it?"

"We're both businessmen, right?" Recker said. "We're just conducting a transaction that benefits the both of us. That's what it's all about, isn't it?"

"Yeah, maybe. Everyone's putting in sealed bids, though. What if someone bids higher?"

"You just have to make sure that I'm declared the winner. Whatever the winning bid is, I'll match it, and kick in another five after that."

"You sound like you want this merchandise pretty bad."

"I do. I have big plans, and this will go a long way to securing those."

"What kind of plans?"

"My business," Recker answered.

"This would create some concerns on the part of the seller. He likes to know who he's doing business with."

"Tell him John Smith. Sixty-plus million should be enough to quell any concerns of his."

"We still need to meet first."

"Where and when?"

"Let's make it two hours from now."

"OK. Where?"

"I'll text you the address to this number when it's time."

"OK."

The line went dead, as Recker pulled the phone away from his ear. He looked at it for a second, thinking about the conversation they just had.

"Well?" Haley asked.

"We meet with him two hours from now."

"Where?"

"He didn't say," Recker replied.

"Then how are we gonna meet?"

"He's gonna text me when it's time."

"Smart. He's not gonna give us any extra time to prepare for it."

"No, he's not." Recker scratched the back of his head. "But at least it's something."

"It also means we could be walking into just about anything. Especially if he doesn't buy the story you just told him, it could be lights out for us."

Recker sighed. "I know. What other options do we have, though?"

"Not many. But we also don't have to make a bad deal just to make any deal."

"Let's just see the place he gives us. Once we go, if we get bad vibes, we can abort when we get there. Let's just take it one thing at a time."

"I'm good with that."

"And the first thing is just getting a meeting. And one's all we need."

"Assuming he doesn't have fifty men with him. Then we'll need more."

"Yeah," Recker said. "But first things first. Right now, we're at the plate. Once we get there, then we'll work on hitting the home run."

14

Instead of just sitting in the car for the next two hours, Recker called Jones again, hoping that he could somehow trace the call that he just had. Maybe they could get lucky and figure out where Webb was this time. Recker figured it was another longshot, but it needed to be checked.

"How are we looking?" Recker asked, hearing Jones feverishly typing in the background.

"When I know, you'll know."

"Well does it look promising or not?"

"Unless I say otherwise, assume not."

"So what you're saying is these guys are better than you?"

"Pushing my buttons, Michael, is not the way to get this done."

"I was just saying."

"If your intent is to rile me up by making it seem like these people have better skills than I do, it is not going to work."

"So what will?"

"Nothing," Jones replied. "No matter how great someone's skills are, I can't find something against someone who's taken the necessary precautions from doing so."

"So they're better?"

"I'm going to ignore that because I know you're just trying to rib me."

Recker finally let out a laugh. "Figured it was worth a shot."

"The only shot not worth taking is the one that you don't take."

Recker was silent for a moment. "Wait, what?"

"I don't know. Did I bungle that phrase?"

"I dunno. Doesn't matter." Recker could still hear his partner typing away. "I still hear you pounding away on those keys. You're not coming up with anything."

"It looks the same as before. Signals bouncing everywhere."

Recker sighed, though it wasn't an unexpected result. "I pretty much figured that's what it was gonna be."

"At the risk of sounding like I'm always the voice of resistance..."

"Don't say it. I already know what you're gonna say. I can hear it in your voice."

"What if this whole thing is a sham?"

"I knew you were gonna say that."

"Have you considered the possibilities?"

"Why, yes, David, I have."

"No need to be condescending. I am just asking if you have considered the fact that this might be a setup."

"Yes, I've considered it."

"But you're going to go, anyway?"

"Listen, we aren't in this business to walk away from leads when we get them," Recker said.

"We're not in this business to wind up dead from stupid mistakes, either. We're still not far removed from Paxton getting killed, and Chris almost losing his life at the same time."

"I'm going into this with my eyes wide open. If we get there, and things seem strange, we'll take off."

"You have to admit, I think it's strange that the man's willing to meet with someone he doesn't know the name of, and who just randomly calls him out of the blue. You don't think his alarm bells are raging out-of-control right now?"

"Maybe they are," Recker answered. "I also know money talks, and a lot of people will do stupid and silly things when they think a big payday is attached."

"Nothing about these men indicate to me they are prone to stupid and silly things."

"So what should we do? Nothing?"

"I don't know. But I think we should proceed under the assumption that this is some sort of trap. I find it highly suspicious that he's willing to meet with you just like that."

"You know, there's three things you can always count on in life."

"Can't wait to hear these," Jones said.

"Death, taxes, and you being negative about a plan."

"I hope you're humoring yourself."

"Maybe."

"Joke if you want to. I am simply expressing my reservations about the logistics of this operation. I do not think it is feasible."

"David, I said we're going into this with our eyes wide open. We're not gonna walk in there without some type of plan."

"Oh? And what is your plan?"

"Uh, I don't know yet. Haven't got that far."

"See? You don't have one. You're proceeding on hope instead of your intelligence."

"I am fully aware that this might be a trap."

"You don't even know where this meeting is going to take place," Jones said. "Which means you can't advance scout, you can't get any intel on it, you can't set up beforehand, you can't do anything."

"I'm well aware of those problems."

"But yet you'll still go."

"Because none of those things mean that it's a trap. It just means that Webb is a very careful individual. None of that should come as a surprise."

"Put me on record as saying that I don't think this is a good idea."

Recker sighed. "You're on record. You're always on record."

"I just want to make sure my opinion is heard before you discard it."

"For the record, since we're talking about it, your opinion is not always discarded. It's valued, it's considered, it's heard, and then we push it aside."

"Very funny. I have valid objections."

"Believe me, I know you do. And you're right for thinking them. And I want you to think of them. And I want you to express those concerns. It helps to consider all possibilities."

"And you're still going to go?"

"As of now, yes."

"As of now? What would make you change your mind?"

"You finding him before we do," Recker answered. Now it was Jones that sighed. "Was that not a good answer?"

"Let's just move on, shall we?"

"Works for me."

"So do you have any plan for when you meet with him? Assuming a meeting actually takes place."

"I thought we were moving on?"

"We are. To a new question."

"Oh. Yeah. I've got a little plan."

"Which is?"

"Once we see him... shoot him." Jones loudly sighed again, making sure his friend heard him. "I take it you have a new objection?"

"I should have known that was your plan," Jones said. "That's always your plan."

"No, it's not."

"When in doubt, just shoot. We should make it a slogan and put it on a t-shirt."

"Not a half-bad idea. But in any case, what should be my objective? Talk to him for a few hours first? If he's like Corbyn, he ain't gonna give away any information freely. Unless, of course, you'd like me to bring him back for questioning at headquarters? Maybe we can try some CIA-level interrogation techniques. Maybe some good old-fashioned waterboarding, huh? Would that tickle your fancy?"

"No, no, do it your way. You always do. Just go in there with your guns blazing. I'm sure Webb will just be standing there in the middle of the room with his arms out to his side, waiting for you to do him in."

"Obviously there will be some other things at play, but we won't know that until we get there, will we?"

"I suppose not."

"Don't worry, David. I've been doing this for a while. I won't just go in there and let myself get blown up. OK?"

"As you wish. I'm going to hang up and try to focus more on this. Maybe I can come up with something."

Recker hung up and looked at his partner. He gave him a shrug.

"He means well," Haley said.

"I know. And I wouldn't ever want him to change. Believe it or not, and he might not, but he helps to keep me honest. Sometimes he says things I need to hear and consider."

Haley smiled. "And in this case?"

Recker looked out the window. "I really hope we're not walking into a trap."

They spent the next couple of hours not doing much except for speculating about what they might be facing. They each watched the time closely, almost counting down until the two-hour mark. Once it hit there, Recker started getting more anxious.

"Over two hours."

"You know something we haven't considered yet?" Haley asked.

"What's that?"

"Maybe Webb doesn't intend to meet us at all. What if he's just using the two hours to get further away, figuring we'd be here waiting for him?"

The look on Recker's face seemed to indicate he thought it was a possibility. "Guess it couldn't be ruled out."

"He could figure the game's up, not trusting anything anymore, and just take off."

Recker kept looking at the time. "I sure hope not."

"But if that puts him on the move, might still give us a chance to pick him up somewhere."

"I just kinda wanna be done with it in either case."

Ten more minutes elapsed, and Recker was starting to get nervous that the text wasn't coming. The more time that went by gave more credence to Haley's thoughts that Webb had no intention of meeting them, and was just using the extra time for his own benefit in escaping.

Then Recker's phone rang. It was the same number that he dialed to talk to Webb. He eagerly answered, putting it on speaker.

"You're late."

"Well, you know how things go," Webb replied. "Things come up, takes time to get things settled. This wasn't exactly on my calendar to start the day, remember?"

"And I thought I was getting a text?"

"Well, texting is so impersonal, don't you think? I mean, I could be texting anyone. This way, I can hear a voice. I know the message was received."

"So where are we meeting?"

"Drive to 107 South Aspen Street."

"What am I looking for when I get there?"

"Nothing. You'll get another call when you get there."

"What's with all the games?"

"Because I don't know you," Webb answered. "So if you really wanna make a deal. This is the game we'll play."

"All right. 107 South Aspen Street."

"Should take you about ten minutes to get there."

"How would you know where we are?"

"You're outside Marci's apartment right now, aren't you?"

Recker shot his partner a look. "Why would we be there?"

"Doesn't matter. If you want this deal, you'll be there in ten minutes. I'll call in exactly ten minutes and you better be there. If you're not, you won't get another call."

Recker motioned to Haley to start driving. "We'll be there."

"Good. Talk to you soon."

As soon as Recker hung up, Haley started peppering him with his thoughts.

"I'm not liking this," Haley said.

"Me neither."

"How's he know we were on Johnson's place?"

"Probably just guessing."

"What if he had someone watching us? What if they're on us now?" Haley looked at his mirrors. "If they are, we ain't got time to lose them."

"I know it."

"This doesn't sound right."

"Let's head to that address and see what happens," Recker said. "If we're still not feeling right, we can call it off."

"OK."

They got to the address in nine minutes. It turned out to be a car wash business. There were a couple of cars in line, but it wasn't overly busy. They sat near the edge of the property, close to the main road, waiting for their next instructions. Exactly one minute later, Recker's phone rang again.

"You made good time."

"What's with the games?" Recker asked.

"Just want to make sure you are who you say you are. Next we'll—"

"No, there's no next. I've got a lot of money burning a hole in my pocket, and I'm not going to play these games. If this is the way you conduct business, then we're out. I'll find someone and somewhere else to spend it. I won't be treated like a bum and run all over town, just hoping you'll find it in your heart to meet me. That's not how I do business."

"OK. Fine. Go to 2238 Stallwood Road. Once you're there, go inside the building and wait."

"Wait for what?"

"Wait for me to get there."

"You won't be there waiting for me?"

"Well I was somewhere else, but since you don't want to play games, we'll cut right to the chase. Just go inside and wait. I'll be there a few minutes after you, probably."

"OK," Recker said. "We'll be there. But if this is another trick, or game, don't bother calling again. Because this deal will be over."

"Don't worry. This is going to be it."

15

Once they arrived at the address that Webb gave them, Haley pulled into the parking lot. There wasn't a single other car to be seen anywhere. Haley parked farther away from the building, not wanting to be too close, just in case something happened. Of course, the case could also be made that parking closer to the building was more beneficial in the event that they had to get out of there in a hurry.

Haley backed into a spot, a solid brick wall behind the parking space, allowing him and Recker to get a full view of the building. They sat there for a few moments, looking at the two-story building. They weren't sure what it was used for, as there were no signs on it, or by the entrance, nothing that would indicate the building was actively in use by any business. But it also wasn't some run-down place that seemed like it was vacant or abandoned. It looked to be in good shape.

Seeing that the glass doors at the front of the building were still intact, they assumed that the place was recently used. Or it hadn't been vacant long enough for people to smash through them yet. Recker and Haley continued sitting there, not moving as they discussed their options.

"I'm not sure I like this," Haley said.

"You're not the only one."

They each looked around, trying to find some sign that someone was nearby. A person, a car, someone looking out one of the windows of the building, anything. But there was nothing. And that was troubling.

"I'm getting that feeling I usually get when something seems off."

"Yeah, I'm getting it too," Recker said.

"So what do you wanna do?"

"Well, we could just wait here for a few minutes, see if Webb actually shows up."

"Yeah, could do that." Haley started looking at the roof of the building, worrying that maybe a sniper was up there, just waiting to pick them off as they exited the car or walked to the building. "What's going through your mind right now?"

"I'm wondering why he wanted us to go in there and wait for him. Not exactly standard procedure for someone you've never met."

"You think he's got a surprise in there for us?"

"Possible."

Recker's phone rang again. It was the same number as before. He quickly answered, once again putting it on speaker for his partner to hear.

"I'm here. I don't see anyone else, though."

"Did you go in yet?" Webb asked.

"No. Don't really see the need to without you being here."

"Well I'm on the way. Got caught in this stupid traffic. Should be about five more minutes. Go inside, kick your feet up. There's coffee, and some other beverages inside. I've got a man in there waiting for you. He'll get you whatever you want until I get there."

Recker continued staring at the building. The feeling that something wasn't right didn't ease up any. "I think I'll just wait until you get here."

"Go inside first."

"Why?"

"Because I still don't trust you. Once you're inside, and my man there gives me the signal that everything's on the up-and-up, then he'll call me and let me know. Once that happens, then I will make my appearance. Not before."

"I told you I don't like the games."

"This is the final one. But if you're not interested in playing, I understand. We can go our separate ways with no hard feelings. But as I said, until I get the signal from my guy in there that everything's good, I will not be there."

"Who is this guy?" Recker asked.

"Someone I trust implicitly. If he believes you're good, then I will believe it."

Recker sighed, still not liking it. But if there was even a chance of them meeting Webb, it seemed it wouldn't happen unless they took that first step. That dangerous and uneasy step.

"So if you want this deal to happen, I need you to go inside and wait for me."

Recker continued staring at the building. "OK. I'll go in and wait. But if you're not here in the next five minutes, I'll be somewhere else by the time you do get here."

"Understood."

Recker put the phone in his pocket.

"Still don't like it," Haley said.

"Neither do I. Still, we can either assume this isn't right and get out of here, and we'll likely never see this guy again, or... we can go in there, and take the chance that this guy's gonna appear in a few minutes."

"That's assuming there isn't something waiting for us in there that's gonna blow us up."

"Yeah."

"I don't like either option."

"I don't either," Recker replied.

"Can't we just take what's behind door number three?"

Recker chuckled. "Don't think so."

"What do you wanna do?"

"Like you say, neither option is very appealing, but we gotta pick one. Right now, I'd rather take the chance that this guy is actually gonna show up. That he's just really cautious."

"If he knows about Corbyn, all these games would make sense," Haley said. "I'm sure he doesn't wanna join the guy."

"I think I should go in and take the risk."

"What about me?"

"Let's walk to the building together," Recker answered. "I'll go in by myself. You stay on the outside and keep a lookout. Make sure nothing's happening out here that I should know about."

"You'll be in there by yourself, though."

"Well, if Webb's to be believed, there's only one guy in there. And I'll be armed. I think it's better than both of us walking in there."

Haley nodded. He was willing to go along with whatever Recker wanted. "OK. I'll keep the wolves at bay out front."

"Let's just hope this goes nice and smooth and all these fears we have are just a byproduct of our secret agent days."

They both checked their weapons, then got out of the car and started walking towards the building. They kept their eyes peeled, looking everywhere to make sure they weren't being set up. They looked at the front door, the roof, the windows, the rest of the parking lot, the entrance to see if any other cars were pulling up, everywhere. There were no outward signs of problems, though.

Once they got to the front of the building, Recker tugged on the glass door, easily pulling it open. Before going in, he looked inside, waiting to see if someone was there waiting for him. There wasn't. He gave Haley a nod, then walked in.

Haley stationed himself just outside the door, standing there like he was the bouncer at a club, not letting anyone inside who shouldn't have been there. His head was constantly moving, looking for the first sign of an issue.

As Recker moved through the building, he kept his hand on his gun, ready to pull it at any second. He was getting the feeling that Haley's initial fears were right about this. Everything felt off.

Recker's eyes danced around the room, looking for anything that stood out. Nothing did. He kept moving. There was the option to go left, right, or straight ahead, which eventually led to the stairs to go to the second floor.

"Anyone here?!" Recker shouted.

He then heard a noise from upstairs. It sounded like a window breaking. Recker hurried to the steps, taking his gun out in the process, and proceeded to go up to the second floor. Once he got up the steps, he took a quick look around before going anywhere. Almost immediately, he started smelling something.

Recker stuck his nose in the air to get a better whiff of it. "Smells like a gas leak."

He didn't need to think too much longer about what was going on here. There was nothing else to check there. The only thing left to do was get out of there as quickly as possible. Recker raced down the steps. The odor was getting stronger by the second.

Recker flew out the front door, Haley in the same spot as when he left. "Get to the car! Gas leak!"

Haley instantly started running as well. They were about three-quarters of the way to the car when they heard a loud bang, then an explosion which knocked the both of them off their feet. After a few seconds of composing themselves, they both got back to their knees, just looking at the building. It was engulfed in flames now.

"What the hell happened in there?" Haley asked.

Recker looked at his partner. "You all right?"

Haley stood up and dusted himself off. "As good as can be, I think. No new holes."

Recker tapped him on the arm. "C'mon. Let's get in the car and get out of here."

They both immediately jumped into the car and left the scene. They had a few minutes before the first responders showed up. As they drove out of the parking lot and onto the street, Haley had questions.

"How did we get to this point?"

"The whole thing was a trap," Recker answered.

"What was with blowing up the building?"

"Pretty sure we were supposed to be inside."

"How'd you know?"

"Smelled the leak."

"Right away? Took a few minutes."

Recker then thought about it. He didn't smell it at first. It wasn't until he reached the second floor. That had to be deliberate planning, he thought. "I didn't smell it at first. It wasn't until I heard a sound from upstairs."

"What kind of sound?"

"Sounded like a window breaking or something. Then when I went up the stairs, that's when I smelled it."

"If it was bad, you would've smelled it right away."

"I know."

"Even if someone was up there waiting for you, then they broke a line, the place wouldn't blow up that fast."

Recker agreed. "Not unless they had something else there to make sure that it did."

"A bomb or something."

Recker nodded, trying to get everything clear in his head. "I initially called out for someone. Nobody answered. Then I heard the noise and went up."

"Once they knew you were inside, they wanted to lure you upstairs. Probably hoping you wouldn't have enough time to escape."

"Yeah, could be. If someone was up there, though, they didn't have a lot of time to escape the blast either."

"They probably had that all worked out. Probably someone standing by a window with a rope or something, then made the noise and jumped down. When he heard you, he activated a timer. Had a car already on and waiting to go."

"Or they were watching from a distance and were doing everything remotely."

"Yeah, that could be too," Haley said. "Either way, the whole thing was a sham. They didn't trust us at all."

"Yeah, that's for sure. I walked right into this one."

"Can't beat yourself up over it. You just went where the clues took us."

"Nah, I was getting too antsy. I wanted it to go faster than we were ready for. Now these guys are in the wind."

"To be fair, they were probably in the wind already. Webb didn't trust you from the start. Nothing you could say or do was gonna change that. Whether we came here or not, his plans weren't changing."

"Yeah, but now... maybe I shouldn't have called to begin with."

"It was the right play," Haley said. "David's not getting anything on his end. This was the right move. Webb's just outplaying us right now."

"I don't see how we're gonna pick him up now."

"Well, like you said before, if he thinks we're on

him, now he's probably gonna be on the move. If he's on the run, moving before he was ready, he might make a mistake."

Recker shook his head slightly, not sure if he bought that. "Not sure if these guys make mistakes."

"They all do. That's how they get caught."

"I guess now we just have to hope they make one."

"In my view, they already have."

"What do you mean? What mistake did they already make?"

"We've already talked to her," Haley replied. "She's no pro. And she knows more than she's saying."

Recker nodded, agreeing. "I guess we should go shake the tree and hope something will fall out of it."

"It will." Haley gave him a grin. "It will."

16

On the way back to Marci Johnson's place, Recker was avoiding calling Jones to let him know what happened. He was dreading the call, mostly because he hated admitting that he was wrong and Jones was right. He did try calling Webb again, though. Not that he was expecting to make some type of deal or meeting or anything. That ship had sailed.

But Recker was hoping to give the man a few lasting words of the threatening variety. Maybe he could have gotten Webb to lose his temper and say something he'd regret. Something to indicate where he was or where he was going. Unfortunately, Webb wasn't picking up. Recker kept trying multiple times, but there was no answer. The ship really had sailed by now.

"No use beating your head against the wall," Haley said. "He's not picking up."

Split Scope

"I guess I was just hoping to get a last word in."

"No luck with that. Hate to say this, but maybe you shouldn't have bothered. Now he knows we're still alive and still coming. At least before, he might have thought we were dead and dropped his guard."

"If this was some amateur, I might agree with you. But this guy, I'm sure he had someone watching that building and reporting back to him about what happened. I'm sure he knows we got away."

"Yeah, you're probably right about that. Wishful thinking, I guess."

"A lot of it going around," Recker said.

"When are you gonna make that other call?"

"What other call?"

"The one to David." Haley let out a laugh. "I know you're avoiding it."

"Shows that much, huh?"

Haley shrugged. "Eh, I dunno. He won't rib you too hard."

"It's not the ribbing I'm dreading."

"Just knowing he was right and rubbing it in your face?"

"Something like that."

"Gonna have to bite the bullet sometime. Might as well just get it over with."

Recker sighed. "Yeah." He looked at his phone again, then started dialing Jones' number.

Jones picked up on the first ring. "How did it go?"

"Uh, not quite as well as I hoped it would."

"Oh? Were there problems? Did you meet Webb?"

"Yes, and no."

"What kind of answer is that?"

"There were problems, and we didn't meet him."

"I get the feeling you are trying to be evasive."

"Probably because I am," Recker said.

"Just come out with it."

"OK, well, we went to the building that Webb told us about, and I went inside, then the place blew up." There was silence on the other end of the phone for about ten seconds. Recker finally tired of waiting. "Um, are you there?"

"Yes, I am here."

"No response."

"When we talked about things blowing up, I really didn't think we were talking about the building literally blowing up."

Recker laughed. "Yeah, news to me too."

"And here you are laughing about it."

"Should I cry?"

"No, you should have listened to me to begin with and not put yourself in that situation."

"I'm sorry, Dad."

"I hate it when you do that."

"What?"

"Get sarcastic with me when you're trying to avoid being yelled at."

Recker sighed. "I know. I'm sorry. You were right. I was overzealous. I shouldn't have gone. I should've waited longer. There. Is that better? Is that what you want to hear?"

"Well, I guess so. I take it you and Chris are all right? No broken bones or anything?"

"We're fine. Just annoyed that we got suckered."

"Look, I understand why you went. I know there is a time element in play here. We just can't afford to make rash decisions that might not be beneficial for us. If they get away or move on before we're able to get to them, we'll just have to live with that. I would much rather have that than rush into something we are not adequately prepared for."

"I agree. We'll be more careful."

"Good. Now that this is hopefully behind us, do you have a next step in mind?"

"Unless you've miraculously come up with something unexpected, we're on our way back to Johnson's."

"For what?" Jones asked. "Hoping that Webb might be dumb enough to swing by?"

"No. We're gonna take our swing at Johnson for another round of questions."

"You really think she'll give up more than she did before?"

"I think there's more that she knows, yeah."

"Knowing and telling are two different things."

"We were trying to tiptoe around things before," Recker said. "That cat's out of the bag. Now it's time to bring out the heavy guns."

"You're going to shoot her?"

"Just a metaphor, David, just a metaphor. I don't really plan on shooting her. Well, not unless I have to, anyway."

"Let's hope it doesn't come to that."

"And if she's got nothing interesting worth sharing? What then?"

"I dunno. I haven't thought that far yet. If she doesn't have anything, maybe we switch tactics and put our efforts on Harris or the other guy."

"The other guy is Rory Zouch."

"Yeah, that's the one."

"I am still looking for them already," Jones said. "Unfortunately, they have not come across my radar yet, so I'm not sure that will be an effective strategy either."

"Well we gotta do something."

"Yes, I know. Don't forget, we are coming into this a little late in the game. We weren't involved from the first inning."

"Shouldn't matter. We're supposed to be closers. Let's close it."

"I'll continue doing what I can from my end. Let me know how your talk goes with Ms. Johnson."

"Will do."

After they hung up, Recker put his phone back in his pocket.

"Didn't sound so bad," Haley said.

Recker raised his eyebrows. "Painful. It's just in his voice. When he knows he's right, it's just in his voice."

Haley laughed. "He's really not that bad."

"Yeah, maybe so. I just hate knowing he's right and I'm wrong."

"Happens. Can't bat a thousand all the time."

"Right now I feel like I'm at the Mendoza Line."

They finally arrived back at Johnson's apartment building, parking near the same spot as they did before, across the street.

"Well, let's go see if we can change that," Haley said with a grin.

They got out of the car and went across the street, keeping their eyes open, just in case Webb and his friends decided to watch the place, too. They doubted he would return and put himself in danger like that, but they couldn't rule it out, either. Haley got to the door first, opening it, and letting his partner go in before him. They went to the steps and started climbing.

"Can't wait to see what kind of reception we'll get this time," Haley said.

Recker laughed. "I'm sure it'll be a doozy."

"No doubt."

Once they got to Johnson's floor, they walked straight to her apartment, with Recker knocking on the door. They took a step back and to the side, making sure they weren't directly in front of it in case Johnson went full-on crazy and started blasting through the door. It wasn't what they expected, but it's been known to happen.

After waiting a few seconds, Recker knocked on the door again, a little harder this time. There was still no answer. Recker and Haley looked at each other. Then Recker put his ear up to the door to see if there was movement inside. He couldn't hear anything.

"Think she flew the coop?" Haley asked.

Recker didn't verbally respond. He just shrugged. He kept listening, though there wasn't a sign of anything inside. It didn't sound like anyone was moving around, no noises from a TV or radio, no voices, nothing. He put his fist up to the door one more time and pounded away four times.

"Johnson," Recker said. "Open up. We wanna talk to you." He kept listening. "I'm not sure anyone's in there."

He then reached down and put his hand on the knob of the door. He slowly started turning it to see if the door was open. It was. He was just about to push it open when Haley put his hand on his partner's arm.

"You sure you wanna do that?"

"Why not?" Recker asked.

"We're dealing with people who know how to blow things up, and have shown they're not afraid to do so. What if you open that door and we blow this building apart?"

Recker looked down at the knob. He hadn't initially considered it, but he couldn't argue with Haley's logic. If Webb anticipated them coming back here, it was possible he had another surprise waiting for them. A lump went down Recker's throat, not sure if he should push that door open further or not.

Recker sighed and looked at Haley again. "You really think they'd blow this place up?"

"Why not?" Haley replied.

"Blowing up an empty building is one thing. A multi-floor apartment building with a bunch of people living in it is something else entirely."

"Yeah, you might be right about that." Haley smiled. "I just thought I'd mention the possibility."

"Well, someone's eventually gonna have to go through this door."

Haley continued smiling. "Like I said, just thought I'd mention it."

"Yeah. You, uh, wanna go outside or something before I go in? I can call you again once it's safe?"

"Nah, I'm good."

"You're sure?"

"Yeah, if we're gonna go up, might as well go up together."

"Rather cavalier from someone who was just fighting for their life in a hospital not too long ago, eh?"

"Canadian now?"

Recker gently pushed the door open all the way. He walked inside, almost like he was walking on eggshells. He was relieved that nothing was going off, blowing up, or shooting at him. Haley followed him inside.

They both had their guns out, just in case they weren't alone.

"Marci," Recker shouted as he looked around. He headed for the kitchen.

Haley went in the other direction toward the bedrooms. "Johnson?"

As Recker turned the corner of the half-wall that separated the kitchen from the living room, he stopped in his tracks, seeing the body of Marci Johnson lying there on the floor.

"Chris!"

Recker knelt beside the body to feel her pulse as Haley came rushing over. The blood that was around the body, soaking up the floor, told them all they needed to know, though. There was a pool of blood around her head and shoulders. She also had three bullet holes in her. Two in the chest, and one in the head. Recker stood up next to his partner as they both looked at the body.

"Looks like she's not telling us anything now," Recker said.

"Sure doesn't look like it."

Recker slapped his leg in frustration. "Oh, well."

"A little excessive, don't you think?" Haley asked. "First one probably killed her. The other two were just for effect."

"Not excessive if you're trying to make a point."

"This was Webb's way of saying you don't mention him to anybody."

Recker nodded. "Yeah."

"Also means we're not too far away from them. This was recent."

"Her body's still warm. They were just here."

"I'll get David on the phone," Haley said. "Maybe he can pick something up on a camera nearby."

"Good idea. I'm gonna start looking around, see if I can find something interesting. Maybe get another lead."

As Haley called Jones, Recker started his search in the kitchen. He looked through the cabinets, the refrigerator, the appliances, and every jar that he could find to see if there was something there. He wasn't sure what he was looking for. He'd probably know when he found it, though. Maybe it was a book, a piece of paper, a journal, anything that would give them something else to go on. Someplace else to go. Something else to investigate.

Of course, it was possible, and maybe even likely, that there wasn't anything. It stood to reason that Webb would've searched the apartment before leaving. But what if he missed something? Or what if he didn't think there was anything to look for? Whatever the case, Recker had to search. Besides, they really didn't have anywhere else to go at the moment.

Once Recker's search in the kitchen was done, he went into the living room, and started turning the place inside out. A few seconds later, Haley joined him.

"David's starting to look at cameras. Maybe he'll pick up something."

"Hopefully we will too," Recker said.

"Anything yet?"

"No."

"I'll start in the bedroom," Haley said.

After he was done in the living room, Recker went into the bathroom since his partner had the bedroom covered. He checked the shower, behind the toilet, under the sink, and rifled through the medicine cabinet. There were a bunch of small bottles and boxes in there, mostly of aspirin, bandaids, allergy medication, or various other things. Recker picked up each bottle for a second, then put them back. Until he got to one aspirin bottle. It felt lighter than the others.

He picked it back up again, then shook it next to his ear. There were no pills inside. He twisted off the cap and looked in it. There was a small piece of paper inside. Recker tried to grab it, but couldn't fit his fingers in to get it. He looked back at the medicine cabinet, seeing a small set of tweezers on the shelf. He grabbed them and put them inside the aspirin bottle, successfully grabbing the paper with them. He took the paper out of the bottle and unfolded it. It was no bigger than a notepad to begin with, that was folded over a few times.

Recker looked at the paper and read it, not that there was much to it. It was just a name and a phone number. It might not have been anything. It might not have had anything to do with what they were working on at the moment. But it was something. And it was big enough that Johnson felt like she had to hide it. Now they just had to figure out whether it was connected to Webb at all.

Haley appeared in the frame of the door. "Bedroom's all clean." He noticed his partner looking at the paper. "What's that?"

Recker handed it over to him. "See for yourself."

Haley read the name. "Eamon Kaiser. Who's this guy?"

"I don't know. For some reason, though, she thought he was important enough to hide this in an aspirin bottle."

"Maybe we're in business, then."

Recker nodded, hoping that was the case. "Maybe we're in business."

17

Lawson was called in for a meeting with her immediate supervisor, Darren Waggener. She entered his office, already having an idea about what this might have been about. Waggener was sitting behind his desk, and looked up at her as she came in. He pointed to the chair in front of the desk.

"Have a seat, Shelly." He opened a file folder that was immediately in front of him. "What are you working on right now?"

"Various things."

"I'm gonna cut right to the chase here. Do you happen to be trying to run down leads on where four ex-MI6 agents might be?"

"No, why?"

"Because you were told to stay off it."

"And I am."

Split Scope

"Then why have I been told you're looking into them?"

"I'm only looking into them as it pertains to an overseas drug shipment that I've heard chatter about."

"What chatter?"

Lawson shrugged. "It's just that. Chatter. I'm trying to figure out if it's legitimate or not."

"You're not trying to find these guys here?"

"I was told to stay away from them, and I am. That doesn't mean I'm going to look away at any piece of information that comes across my desk that pertains to them."

"And how does this chatter pertain to them?"

"I've heard that they are here as intermediaries, looking to set up a major drug shipment. I've been told that this shipment may be originating from Pakistan. I think it may wind up traveling to the UK, then coming here. This all may be happening within the next two months."

Waggener sighed and ran his hands over the front of his face. There was clearly something else on his mind. He cleared his throat, looking at the contents of the file folder in front of him.

"Do you happen to know anything about Piers Corbyn?"

"Other than the fact he murdered one of our own?"

"He was killed a short time ago. In Newark."

"Oh," Lawson said, a fake look of shock on her face. "That's just a terrible shame. I feel so bad for him."

"Did you have anything to do with that?"

"How could I? I was told to stay away from it. And I'm completely in the dark about anything that's happening."

Waggener gave her a look. "Shelly, you were pulled away from it because we were concerned about your objectivity."

"My what?"

"Listen, we all want these scumbags to pay for what they did, but there are other things in play that have to prevent what we would like to be the outcome for them."

"Such as?"

"Look, you're great at what you do. And the Director obviously feels very highly of you, which is why you've been promoted like three different times in the last two years. And one day, you'll probably be running this whole operation, but right now, you need to take a step back."

"I'm not doing anything."

"I'm not sure it's a coincidence that one of the men we've been looking at suddenly drops dead here."

Lawson slightly turned her head and put her hand on her ear. "I may have some theories on that."

"Shelly, you were pulled on this because we thought you were too involved."

"I should just turn a blind eye toward what they did?"

"No. Of course not. But we need them alive right now."

"Why? Why are they so important? Bring me in on what you know and maybe I can help."

"We need them alive because we already know about that drug shipment. We've known about it for months."

"For months?"

"We already got wind that there was a big shipment coming from overseas. What we didn't know was who, or where."

"Well we know about these guys," Lawson said.

"They're not the ones behind it. They're the muscle. We need to know where this shipment is coming from. And beyond that, we believe the shipment is already here."

"What? Already here? No, that can't be. I was expressly told that the shipment is coming in two months."

"Who told you that?"

"I can't say."

"Look, we believe the shipment did come from Pakistan via the UK, and then came into New York. We think that shipment came in over two weeks ago."

"Just before the crew arrived here?"

"Yes. We think part of their being here is guarding the shipment, finding a buyer, and then delivering. It's a big haul, probably close to fifty million."

"Then why are they saying it's not coming for two months?"

"Who's saying that?"

Lawson sighed. "Look, I had someone meet with Corbyn before he got killed. Corbyn told him the shipment wasn't coming for two months."

"I think that was a misdirection on their part. And you had someone meeting with them?"

"I just wanted to know what was going on. And since I wasn't being told…"

Waggener wiped the side of his face. "Shelly."

"I can help on this."

"Do you have people working on this off the books?"

Lawson cleared her throat. "I… might possibly."

Waggener threw his hands up. "Shelly, what are you doing?"

"If you just bring me in, I can help. As long as the end goal is eliminating these bastards at some point after we figure out who's behind this shipment, I can hold off on them for now."

Waggener coughed. "OK. Fine. You're in." He reached over for another file folder and slid it over to her. "But whoever you've got on this, call them off."

"No, they're making progress."

"Who do you have working on this?"

"Uh, I can't say."

"Are they with the agency?"

"Not now."

"If something happens, it can't come back to us."

"It won't," Lawson said. "They know how to operate. Believe me, I wouldn't have brought just anybody into this. They're the best."

"Did they kill Corbyn?"

"Not directly, no. That was… someone else."

"But you know who?"

"Maybe. But it wasn't my doing."

"OK. I'm just telling you, those other three cannot be killed yet. We need to use them to track down whoever's behind this shipment. Even if we kill them, the person in charge of this will still be out there. And in a few months, there'll be another shipment. And another one after that. And after that. That's what we have to prevent here."

"Understood." She saw a look on his face that indicated he wasn't quite sure. "Really. I do."

"In regards to these operators you have out there, how much do they know? And are they trustworthy?"

"Completely trustworthy. They've worked for the agency before. They know how things work."

"Are they still in good standing?"

"They are."

"Should I assume it's Cain and Raines?"

"You should not," Lawson answered. "Because it's not."

"Fine. I'm not gonna press you on it, as long as you're sure they can be controlled."

"Oh, definitely. No issues there."

"Good. Now go out there and look through that folder. You learn anything that's not already there, I want to know about it."

"Will do. And thank you."

"Just make sure I won't regret bringing you in on this."

"You won't. I promise. Mission first."

∼

Recker and Haley were back in their car, though they hadn't driven away from Johnson's apartment yet. Recker got on the phone with Jones, hoping he could help with finding out who Eamon Kaiser was.

"David, need you to find out everything you can on Eamon Kaiser."

"And who is he supposed to be?" Jones asked.

"No idea." Recker then read his phone number. "Don't even know if he's related to this case. But I found his name and number on a piece of paper stuffed in an empty aspirin bottle in Johnson's medicine cabinet. Seems to me he might be important somehow."

"He might just be another connection of hers."

"Could be. But if he's important enough to try and hide, maybe he's important enough for us to look into."

"I'll start pulling up his info and I'll call you back in a few minutes."

"I'll eagerly be waiting."

After Recker hung up, he and Haley started discussing their next options.

"I feel like we should be doing something," Haley said.

"Maybe Kaiser's the next piece."

"What's your gut say?"

Recker shook his head, not having a clear handle on it. "I don't know. The guy's obviously important somehow. You don't shove his name in an aspirin bottle because he's just the neighborhood junk dealer, do you?"

"Wouldn't think so."

"Maybe he's somehow tied to Webb. Maybe another contact. Maybe a go-between. Or maybe he's… just some random person. I'd like to think we hit pay dirt and we can get to Webb through him, but somehow, I get the feeling we won't be that lucky."

"That would be something. Not sure Webb would like her hiding an important name like that around her apartment if they were involved, though."

"Maybe that's why she did it," Recker replied. "Some sort of protection against Webb. Or maybe she's using the name to hang over Webb's head for some reason. Nothing but conjecture until we find out who the guy is."

"I'm gonna start driving."

"To where?"

"I dunno. Anywhere but here. Isn't that the saying?"

"Yeah. Probably a good idea anyway. Who knows if they called the cops after they did it? Even if they didn't, there'll probably be a swarm of them coming in soon enough. Best if we get some distance between us."

They were on the road for about ten minutes when Jones called back. Recker anxiously answered, hoping he had some gold nuggets of information for them.

"I'm assuming you've cracked the case wide open with what you've found?"

Jones was quiet for a few moments before answering. "I'm sure you're either intentionally overly optimistic or you're being sarcastic in thinking I found nothing. I'm not sure which."

"Why couldn't it be both at the same time?"

"Yes, probably more realistic, isn't it?"

"So, did you find anything?"

"Of course," Jones replied.

"Anything of value?"

"Would I call you if there wasn't?"

"Uh… maybe."

"Anyway, I've looked up Mr. Kaiser and I've found several disturbing things."

"Disturbing for who?"

"Would you just let me explain?"

"Proceed," Recker said.

"So Mr. Kaiser is forty-seven years old, and has a lengthy criminal history. And he's been arrested for quite a bit, though not always charged. He's been in prison twice."

"Sounds like a swell guy."

"He seems to have a penchant for violence, as well."

"OK? How does he tie in with Johnson?"

"That part I have not figured out yet. Maybe there's something in their backgrounds that would indicate the connection, but it's not obvious at the moment."

"Could he have a connection to Webb?" Recker asked.

"Can't ascertain that yet, either. It's possible. I don't know if it's likely. I've done a few basic preliminary checks, but nothing that reached out for further investigation."

"Who's Kaiser got ties to? Anyone in particular?"

"On the outset, he looks like a freelancer."

"So he's a freelancer, Webb's a freelancer, the other guys are freelancers. It's a lot of freelancers."

"So it seems."

"All right, keep me posted if you find out anything else, I guess."

"I certainly will," Jones said.

"And send me his address."

"On its way."

Once Recker got off the phone, he relayed the information to Haley. He got the text message with Kaiser's address, and he gave it to his partner so they could head over there.

"You think this guy's involved?"

"I dunno," Recker answered. "I just have a feeling.

It's just the hiding his name in the bottle that concerns me. You don't do that unless the guy's a big deal, and you don't want anyone to know about him."

"But it could be a big deal concerning someone else other than Webb."

"Yeah, I know." Recker thought a little more about it. "Wait, didn't Johnson tell us that she sometimes delivered packages, or passed envelopes to people?"

"Yeah."

"Maybe Kaiser's one of the guys that Webb had her passing stuff to."

"Guess that could be," Haley said. "I got another one."

"What's that?"

"Maybe Johnson knew more than she was supposed to know. Saw some things she wasn't supposed to see. Maybe she saw Webb and Kaiser together or something. Found out his name and phone number. You know, the whole saving information for blackmail later on type of deal?"

"You mean she'd try to blackmail Webb about Kaiser?"

Haley shrugged. "Just a thought. Might explain why she was killed."

"Possible. I have a feeling she was killed because of us, though. I don't think he trusted her to keep quiet if we came back to her."

"Probably more likely."

"Can't really deny anything at this point, though. How long until we get to his place?"

Haley looked at the GPS. "About twenty minutes or so. Assuming he's still there, and that's his actual address. What do you wanna do when we get there?"

"Just play it by ear, I guess. And hope for the best."

18

Recker and Haley were only two or three minutes away from the address they had on Kaiser. Then Jones called.

"What's up?" Recker asked. "Got anything else?"

"What I have is a different address."

"Say that again?"

"The address you're going to is bogus."

"How do you know?"

"Because I've been running down that phone number you gave me," Jones said.

"Oh. So how do they connect?"

"The number on that phone comes back to a different name."

"So it doesn't belong to Kaiser?"

"It does. It belongs to an alias he's used before."

"But not the house?"

"No," Jones answered. "Forget about the house,

OK? Just trust me. He's not there. It comes back to someone else."

"How can it come back to someone else? Aren't you the one who told us he was there to begin with?"

"Yes, but... it's long and complicated, OK? Just listen and understand what I'm telling you. He's not there. Just accept that and move on."

"To what? You haven't told me anything else."

"I've been tracking down that number and digging into phone records for it."

"And?" Recker said, hoping he was about to get something big and juicy.

"I've been able to track the phone to an IP address another fifteen minutes away from where you are."

"Fifteen minutes?"

"At least it's in the same state."

Recker sighed. "Send the address to Chris so he can pivot in that direction."

Jones did, then continued talking about his new findings. "Interestingly enough, I've also been able to connect that phone number of Kaiser's to the same one that you called Webb with."

"Wait, you're saying Kaiser has called Webb?"

"Yes, and the best news is that the last call happened yesterday."

"For how long?"

"About eight minutes."

"Interesting," Recker said. "So they're doing some kind of business together."

"It would appear. I've also tracked twelve other calls in the last three months."

"I guess the question is whether they're talking about this big shipment, or whether they're discussing something else?"

"That I can't answer."

"Well can you answer whether Kaiser is actually at this new place you're telling us to go to?"

"He was as of six minutes ago. He made a call to another number."

"Who?"

"Still working that out," Jones replied. "He's got a very lengthy call history. I'm going through the numbers now and writing the names down. I recognized Webb's number right away. That's why I called. Along with the fact that he was somewhere else."

"OK, thanks."

"When you get there, please use some caution. As I said, Kaiser has a violent history. I sincerely doubt you'll be able to knock on the door and pretend you're a salesman to get some answers."

"So come up shooting? Got it."

"That's not what I'm saying! I'm saying use restraint."

"Got it," Recker said. "Use restraint, then fire."

"Oh my, why do I bother?"

Recker laughed, then hung up. He looked over at his partner. "You got the address?"

"Yeah, we're heading there," Haley said. "About twelve more minutes."

"Hope he doesn't call back before we get there and send us somewhere else."

"Almost like playing that whack-a-mole game. Just going from one place to another, not sure where the next one's gonna pop up."

"Let's just hope we can nail this one over the head."

They were only a few minutes away from Kaiser's place when Recker's phone rang again.

"You sure are hitting the top of the popularity charts these days, aren't ya?" Haley said.

"Yeah, you know me. I love to be popular." Lawson's name appeared on the ID, and he answered the phone. "Hey, what's up?"

"I've got some news for you," Lawson said.

"Just what I like to hear."

"I've been clued in to everything here."

"What? You're on the case now?"

"Yeah. I think they got wind of me snooping around on some things. I guess they figured it was better to have me with them and not screwing things up as opposed to doing things on my own and messing up what they've got going on."

"Which is?" Recker asked.

"They want these last three guys alive. Well, at least one of them, anyway. They want the guy who's behind this shipment. If all these guys get killed now, we might not get that. And get this... it's believed that big shipment of drugs is already here."

"Already here? That's not the intel we've got."

"Corbyn must've been lying about the timeline. Like I said, I've been briefed and have been looking at a folder full of info, and it looks pretty solid. Tracing everything back, it looks like there was something that can be traced from Pakistan, to the UK, then coming into New York. That shipment came in several weeks ago."

"I would say it sounds easy enough to just go to where that ship came in and find the stuff, but I'm assuming it's not that simple."

"It's not," Lawson said. "It's been checked. The merch was already moved by the time we got there."

"And no idea where it went after that?"

"No. Could've gone anywhere in a dozen different directions."

"Could be it's one of the cities those four flew into."

"Maybe. It's also possible they deliberately flew into those locations knowing the shipment's not there, just in case they were found out."

Recker sighed. "So what are you saying? Abort the previous plans?"

"I'm saying... based on what I've been told, it would be extremely helpful if we could find out who's behind this before these guys get taken out."

"So ask questions first before they get killed? That's what you're saying?"

Lawson laughed. "Well, it's kind of tough to get information out of a dead body, isn't it?"

"I dunno. Seems like maybe it's been done before."

"Well if you could develop that technique further, you could probably make a lot of money selling the secrets."

"Tempting offer. So you have any other tidbits you'd like to share since you're in the know now?"

"No, just a bunch of names that need to be cross-referenced on our end. Not a lot else is known about all of this other than the fact we've traced a shipment, though it's a few weeks too late to do anything about that. And the fact that we know these guys are here. Everything else is still unknown. But the big one... is who's behind all this. After we know that, then we can drop these guys."

"OK, well, maybe we'll have something else for you in a little bit."

"Why? You onto something?"

"Maybe," Recker replied. "Not sure yet. Could be a wild goose chase. Just a name that came up when we searched Marci Johnson's place, who's now dead, and we're assuming it's Webb's doing."

"What's the name?"

"Eamon Kaiser."

"Unusual name. But one that seems familiar for some reason."

"You've heard it before?"

"I'm almost sure I've come across it before." Lawson

was sitting at her desk with a bunch of files and papers sprawled out in front of her. She immediately started shuffling things around to find what she was looking for. "Hold on, let me check something here."

Recker could hear things being moved in the background. He couldn't resist a joke while he waited. "Sure, we've got all day here."

Lawson chuckled. "Sarcasm will get you nowhere."

"Wow, you sound just like David."

"Great minds think alike, right?"

"So they say."

Lawson continued shuffling papers around until she found the one she was looking for. "Yeah, here it is. I've found it. And it only took a minute."

"Hey, you know patience is one of my virtues."

"Were you always so impatient?"

"No. As a matter of fact, I used to be a lot more patient in my younger days. It's worn off as I've gotten older. The older I get, the more I hate wasting time. You've only got so much of it left."

"True, true." Lawson kept reading to find what she was searching for.

"How you doing there?"

"Good. Just give me a sec. I'm looking through a list of names here."

"Got mine on there?"

"No. Don't be ridiculous."

"Just thought I'd check."

"Wait, I've got it!"

Split Scope

"Is it catching?"

"Would you stop?" Lawson said. "Is this what David has to put up with most of the time?"

"Usually."

"Oh my gosh, now I know why he always complains about you."

"Just how often do you talk to him?"

"Uh, story for another day. Anyway, I've found him."

"Who?"

"Kaiser."

"Doing what?"

"No, he's on this list I've got."

"Why?" Recker asked.

"He's on the list of names we've got associated with Harris."

"Really? If you know about this guy, then... what are we doing here?"

"I've just been studying this list today," Lawson answered. "Remember, I was sitting on the sidelines until recently. I just spent the last hour going over some of the information they gave me, and I remembered seeing that name."

"What else do you know about him?"

"Suspected of being a connection to several overseas operations. Current whereabouts are unknown."

"Uh, well, they're known now."

"Wait, you know where this guy is?"

"Yeah, we're heading over there now. At least we

think it's him. Don't have a visual confirmation yet. That's what we're doing. Making sure the guy is where we've pinned him down at."

"How'd you get his name?" Lawson asked.

"Name and number was written down and stuffed inside an aspirin bottle in Marci Johnson's apartment. David tracked him down to some other place, but his phone number is giving off signals to this place we're going now."

"Wow, that's big. We have nothing on him other than suspicions. Like, no address, phone number, nothing. He's like a ghost."

"Well, looks like we just pulled the sheet off. In your information there, does it say Kaiser is connected to our MI6 friends?"

"Not to them specifically. He's got ties to several organizations, and it's some of those organizations that we're trying to see if they're behind this. I mean, we've got hundreds of names on this list that may be tied to this."

"Seems kind of fishy that Johnson knows both of them. And David pinpointed calls made between Kaiser and Webb."

"She's gotta be the link, then."

"Seems so," Recker said. "A lot of these groups use people that are under the radar, people nobody would suspect. I think that was Johnson to them. If someone stopped her or looked into her, nobody would think twice about her being involved with these big organizations."

"Especially if it's just to drop off packages and information and the like."

They continued talking until Haley stopped the car, pulling alongside the curb. Recker looked at his partner, who pointed to the building.

"That's it," Haley said.

"Listen, we're here at Kaiser's," Recker said. "I'll call you later."

"OK," Lawson said. "Let me know what happens."

"Will do."

Recker put his phone away, then looked at the house. It was just outside the city, in the suburbs. It looked to be a nice place. A lot of grass and property. And a big house to go with it. There was also a gate at the front entrance, like celebrities or people on the wrong side of the law have, so they don't get unwelcome visitors.

"What do you think?" Haley asked.

Recker continued looking at the house. "I think we're not getting in there without a fight."

19

Recker and Haley spent the next little while going over plans and options. None of them were very appealing.

"That place looks like it's tougher to break in than some banks I've seen," Haley said. "Gates, security cameras, walls, and you just know there's some armed guards in there, too."

"I'd be surprised if there wasn't."

"How are we gonna talk to this guy? Bet there's a couple mean dogs walking around the premises too."

Recker went on his phone and looked up some satellite images of the property, hoping to find some area that looked like it was a good spot to enter. Nothing came to mind, though. There was only one entrance. The rest of the place had a fence around it. And they could already see cameras at the gate, as well as at the corners of the property. However they decided to get in, if they actually tried, they would be seen long before they got to the house.

"One thing's for sure," Recker said. "We can't just sit here and wait for something to break. For one, this guy might not need to talk to Webb again, and might not leave the house in the next few days."

"And two?"

"That was basically it. One was bad enough."

"I got something," Haley said.

"Throw it out there."

"What if we just drive up to the gate and say that Webb sent us?"

"Why would he do that?"

"Could say we've got an important message for him, and Webb didn't want to risk getting tapped on a phone call."

"And what if Kaiser's extra careful and calls Johnson up, just to make sure he sent us?"

Haley laughed. "Then I guess we'd be in trouble. But if he calls that number you got, Webb might not answer because of everything that's happened so far. He might have thrown that phone away."

"What if he's got a different number for Webb? Or Webb already told him about us?"

Haley laughed again. "Like I said, I guess we'd be in trouble again."

"I dunno. I think those options are a little riskier than I'd like."

"I don't see how else we're getting in. Unless we

smash through the front gate and raise a big stink. But then, Kaiser might have time to get away long before we find him. Especially if he has guards. We'll be tied up with them before we even sniff him."

Recker sighed as he kept looking at the house. As it looked now, there was no way to get in without being seen. It just wasn't possible. They could try as Haley suggested, and attempt to finagle their way in somehow, but that brought its own set of risks. As he continued to think about it, there was only one way to get in from his perspective. They had to get in unseen, and take everyone by surprise. And the only way to do that was if the cameras weren't working.

"Think David can kill those cameras?" Recker asked.

Haley shrugged. "Maybe. One sure way to find out."

Recker picked up his phone again and called Jones, who picked up right away.

"Trouble already?" Jones asked.

"No. Well, yeah. Kind of."

"So which is it?"

"We're outside the place you told us, and we do have a slight issue," Recker said.

"Not enough bodies to shoot?"

"Can you stop joking around and listen to me?"

"I'm all ears."

"This place looks like a fortress. Front gate, high walls, security cameras on every corner. I pulled up the satellite images, and it doesn't look any better on the other side."

"So what are you suggesting?"

"I'm not suggesting anything," Recker replied. "I'm asking if you're able to cut those cameras so we can get in unseen."

"What else are we up against?"

"Doesn't matter. Chris and I will take care of whatever else we're up against. The only thing we need from you is figuring out how to get us in there without being seen. Are you able to do that?"

"What kind of cameras are we talking about?"

"I dunno. Regular security cameras, I guess."

"Wireless? Wired? What?"

"Look wireless to me," Recker answered.

"If they're wireless, I should be able to get into them. What do you want me to do, knock them offline?"

"I don't know. Is it better to knock them all off, or just cut off the one we need, that way it looks like just one's malfunctioning?"

"A case could be made in either instance, I believe. If you just cut one, they're probably going to check that one out, meaning they will be coming straight for you. But if you cut them all, that might put their guard up even more, thinking someone's trying something shady. So I guess it really depends on your own instincts."

Recker looked over at his partner for his input.

"I say cut them all," Haley said. "If we cut one, they'll be coming in our direction. Cut them all, they'll still be spread out. Hopefully. And even if they think something funny's going on, they won't necessarily think it's us coming. Might just think it's a hack job, and someone's trying to get into their system remotely."

Recker nodded, appearing like he agreed. "Yeah. Let's go with that. Knock them all out."

"Well, I can probably do that," Jones said. "Just give me a few minutes. I'll call you back when I'm ready."

Recker shook his head, leaving his partner to wonder what was wrong. "What's the matter?" Haley asked.

"It's ridiculous how easy it is to hack into things these days. Especially when it's something like a security camera, which is by default supposed to give you peace of mind."

"Well it works for us in this case."

"Yeah, and it's not them that I worry about. It's the regular people out there who think they're protected and they're really not." While they waited, Recker continued looking at the images of the property, trying to figure out the best point of entry. "Let's swing around to the back, huh?"

"You see a spot?"

Recker showed him the picture. "Right here." He pointed to a part of the fence, where a tree was behind it, on the inside part of the property. "Branches hang low over it. We might be able to tug ourselves up, climb over."

"Let's take a look." Haley started the car and drove around to the other side of the house. They had a good look at the back. They compared the fence with what was shown in the satellite image. "Still there. Those branches don't look that thick, though. Not sure if that'll hold us, or we'll be able to climb up on it."

"We'll need something to boost us up."

"Do it the old-fashioned way? I'll put my hands together and boost you up. Then when you get up there, you pull me up, then away we go."

"Yeah, OK. That should work."

"How are we gonna proceed once we get over that fence, though? Still a little distance between that and the house."

They kept looking over the images. "Going over in this spot, the tree should conceal us for a few seconds. This is the back of the house. There's an in-ground pool there we can get around, and some other bushes there. We can get to the back of the house in ten seconds, maybe?"

"Assuming there's nothing chasing us once we get in there. We might have another problem, though."

"What's that?"

"If we come through the back, who's to say Kaiser won't slip out the front?" Recker rubbed his chin, thinking about it. "Unless we split up. One of us takes the back, the other the front."

"I'm not sure I wanna do that," Recker said. "Without knowing how many people we're dealing with here, who knows what we'll run into? I'd rather us stick together, watch each other's backs, figure it out as we go. If we lose him, we lose him. But I don't wanna lose either of us 'cause we're not prepared for the odds."

Haley nodded, agreeing with that logic. "Works for me."

"Assuming David hacks into this thing at some point."

"He'll get it."

A couple minutes later, Jones called back. Recker eagerly answered.

"How's it looking?"

"It's looking like I'm about to cut out their security system," Jones replied. "All you have to do is tell me when you're ready."

"How long?"

"Until you tell me to get it back online."

Recker looked at his watch. "Give us sixty seconds. Then cut it."

"Starting when?"

"Now." Recker hung up. He and Haley double-checked their weapons. "Let's try to get in there as quietly as possible."

"Let's do it," Haley said.

Split Scope

They waited for the minute to elapse, then got out of their car. Recker and Haley jogged over to the back of the fence, with Haley locking his hands out in front of him to allow Recker to boost himself to the top of the fence. Luckily, it was the type of fence that was wide enough to allow Recker to sit on top of it for a moment in order to help his partner up as well. They both then dropped to the inside part of the property on the grass.

"Love these concrete fences," Haley said. "Much better than the regular ones."

They remained in that spot for a few seconds, spinning their heads around. They heard commotion near the house, probably the guards starting to run around, frantic about the security system getting knocked out. They observed three men coming out of the back of the house and starting to run around to the front. Two of them had guns in their hands.

"Well, there's three," Haley said.

"Yeah. Question is... how many more?"

They waited a few more seconds, then moved around the bush they were currently standing behind. They didn't want to wait too much longer. They started running toward the house, going around the in-ground pool. They kept their eyes peeled for the guards, as well as anyone else that may have been watching. They got to the back of the house unscathed, though.

Recker pulled open the half-glass back door, and waited there for a second, his gun ready to fire at whoever crossed his path. But there was no one there. He rushed inside, Haley right behind him. They quickly started searching rooms, hoping to find Eamon Kaiser.

The first few rooms they went into, they found nothing. It seemed as if the first floor was empty. Maybe everyone was outside, or trying to figure out what happened to the security system, but they weren't challenged yet. Until they reached a door that was closed. Looked like it might have been an office, or a spare bedroom. It was a regular slab door, so they couldn't see inside.

Recker put his ear up to the door, and immediately heard voices. He looked at Haley and nodded, letting him know they were about to get some business. Recker then started putting fingers in the air. One, two, four, then shook his hand slightly. There were at least four different voices that Recker could make out. There might have been more. But four that he could definitely decipher.

Recker put his hand on the knob, ready to open it. He looked at Haley, who gave him a nod, signaling that he was ready to go, too. Recker quickly turned the knob, then pushed the door open. He and Haley went in, their guns in front of them. There were five men sitting around at desks, monitors in front of each of them. Recker wasn't sure if they were the security team, or they had some other task that they worked on.

It didn't matter much, though. Right now, they were in the way.

Four of the men immediately put their hands up, not wanting a fight. Of course, the two guns staring them in the face probably had something to do with that. There was one man, though, like there usually is, that didn't seem bothered by it. He quickly reached into his desk drawer and removed a gun. He sprung up out of his chair, hoping to fire at the two strangers who'd burst into the room. He barely got out of his seat, though, as Recker and Haley each plugged him at the same time, sending him sprawling over his chair and crashing to the floor. The rest of the men kept their hands up, barely moving an inch.

"Anyone else have a problem?" Recker asked. Everyone shook their heads. "Good. We're looking for Kaiser. Tell us where he is and none of you will get hurt."

The seated men all looked at each other, none of whom wanted to be the one to give up their boss' location. Recker could see they were almost as much in fear of their boss, and being labeled as the one to give him up, as they were of the two armed men in front of them. He had to change their mind, and he had to do it quickly. They didn't have time for a long interrogation process here.

"Listen, one of you is gonna tell me what I want to know," Recker said. "And if I have to kill all of you except for one to make that happen, I will. I'd rather not waste the bullets, though."

Still, no one spoke up.

Recker sighed, not wanting to play these types of games. They didn't have time. Each second they wasted here was time that Kaiser might use to get away. As Recker dealt with those men, Haley turned around to keep an eye out, making sure nobody surprised them from behind.

Recker walked up to the nearest desk, and put his gun on the side of the man's temple. "Where is he?" The man gulped. "You've got five seconds, or you'll be the next one to join your friend over there." The man still said nothing. Recker started counting. "One, two, three, four..."

"OK! OK! I'll tell you."

"Now."

"He's upstairs in his office."

"Which is where?"

"Up the steps, go to your right, last door to the left."

"If you're lying to me, I'm gonna come back down here and put a bullet in your head."

"He's there. He should be. He was there ten minutes ago."

Recker seemed satisfied that the man was being honest with him. But now he had another problem. What to do with them? He couldn't just leave them be, or they could tell Kaiser, or the guards outside, and then they'd really be up against it. But Recker didn't want to kill them either. They weren't posing a threat.

He looked around the room, hoping to see some rope or something. There was nothing obvious, and they still didn't have time to waste on these guys. He noticed another door to the side of the room. He hoped it was a closet. Recker walked over to it and opened it. It was a closet.

"All right, you guys, in here," Recker said.

"What?" one of them said.

"You heard me. In here! Let's go! I don't have time for games. You either go in here on your own, or I'll drop you where you stand. Your choice."

The men instantly got up and shuffled toward the closet. They each went in willingly, not that it was a surprise considering the alternative. Once they were all inside, Recker closed the door and locked it. He still didn't feel all that great about the situation, as he felt if they all put their weight into it, they might be able to break the door down. He looked around, and the only thing he saw heavy enough to put in front of the door were the desks.

Recker tapped Haley, and the two of them started moving the desks in front of the door. Just two of them. One on bottom, then another on top of it. That should have been heavy enough to keep the men in there long enough for Recker and Haley to do their thing.

Once that was done, Recker and Haley went back to the door and peeked out.

"Looks good so far," Haley said.

"Yeah. Whether it remains that way's another question."

"I'll be shocked if we don't run into some more opposition."

"You and me both, partner. You and me both."

20

With the coast clear, Recker and Haley sped out of the office and flew up the steps. They were about halfway up, though, when trouble found them at the top. A guard appeared at the top of the steps. As soon as the man saw Recker and Haley coming up, he knew it was trouble.

"Hey!" the guard yelled.

He started reaching for his gun, but Recker stopped and fired before the man was able to remove his weapon. The man fell forward, tumbling down the steps. Recker and Haley moved to the side so as not to get in the man's way and go down with him. They continued their trek up the steps, reaching the second floor. As soon as they made it, they were greeted by another pair of guards.

Recker and Haley each took one, and started wrestling around, as well as throwing some punches.

Recker was able to throw his guy down the stairs, while Haley threw his opponent over the railing, effectively ending each fight.

Before moving on, they each looked for another battle, though there was none coming. At least not at the moment. They continued going down the hall until they got to the last door on the left. It was closed. Recker listened at the door again as Haley stood guard. He couldn't hear anything this time.

Recker turned the handle on the door and pushed it open. Both men rushed inside, guns out and ready to fire. They quickly scanned the room for a target. There was no one there, though. It definitely looked like an office. Haley closed the door, and the two of them stood there, looking at each other.

"What now?" Haley asked.

Recker sighed, and shrugged, not sure himself. He certainly didn't like the prospect of searching the rest of the house. They were bound to run into more trouble. There was nothing else they could do, though. Kaiser wasn't there.

They started for the door again, but just before they were about to open it, Recker thought he heard something. He put his hand on Haley's arm to stop him from leaving.

"What is it?" Haley asked.

"I heard something."

"What?"

"I'm not sure," Recker replied.

"From where?"

Recker shook his head. He didn't know. But he did know he heard something. He took another look around the room. He looked up at the ceiling, the walls, the floor, anyplace that someone could've tried to hide or conceal themselves. Then he took a closer look at the bookshelf that was along the wall, near the desk.

Recker walked over to it. He stood in front of it, staring at it. There was something off about it. He wasn't sure what it was. He just got the feeling it wasn't what it seemed. He thought he detected another noise. It was coming from beyond the bookcase.

Recker reached in and started clearing off the shelves, with books falling to the ground. He had only cleared about half of it when he saw what he was looking for. On the right-hand side, there was a small button, which usually would have been covered up by one of the books.

Before pressing it, he looked at Haley, and nodded, letting him know something was there. He took out his gun again, not sure what they were going to find once the bookshelf opened up. Haley came over to the bookshelf, standing next to his friend. Recker pressed the button, then quickly stepped back. They both stood there, their guns pointed at the bookshelf as it slowly started to move.

Seconds later, the bookshelf stopped moving, revealing a hole in the wall. They had hoped they'd have found Kaiser sitting there, balled up on the floor, waiting to be dragged out. But it wasn't that easy. It was just a hole in the wall. They moved in closer to inspect it, seeing that there were steps.

"Wonder where the hell that goes," Haley said.

"Gotta go down to the basement, doesn't it?"

"But if there's a basement, I don't remember seeing steps that led outside from it, do you?"

Recker thought back to the pictures. "No."

"So what good's it do going to the basement if you can't escape from there?"

Recker kept thinking. "It's gotta go somewhere else, then."

"But where?"

Recker remembered a bookshelf in the living room on the first floor. He then looked at the bookshelf that they were standing next to. They looked identical. "First floor. In the living room, there was a bookshelf that looked just like this one."

"He's escaping through there."

"We gotta head him off!"

Recker and Haley raced out of the room. They sped down the hallway, and flew down the steps. Just as they reached the bottom of the stairs, they looked and saw the bookcase moving. They were about to rush over to it and greet Kaiser, but the front door suddenly swung open. It was the three guards Recker and Haley initially saw in the back when they first came over the fence.

Everyone pointed guns at each other, and in a split-second, gunfire filled the room. All of them were able to get shots off. Recker and Haley's, though, were the only ones that found their targets. The bullets aimed for them narrowly missed, though they could each hear the buzz as the bullets ripped past them, lodging into the staircase.

With Recker and Haley being occupied with the guards, Kaiser was able to slip out of the house. Recker looked at the bookshelf and saw that it was now fully open. Kaiser was on the run.

"Head out the back," Recker said. "Cut him off!"

Haley ran through the back of the house, while Recker stepped over the dead bodies by the front door. Almost immediately after going outside, Recker was met with more gunfire. He leaned over, as bullets ripped into several of the columns in front of the house. Recker quickly got behind one of them for cover, then peeked around it, trying to determine where the shooter was.

As he looked for the shooter, one of the bullets came dangerously close to Recker's face, ricocheting off the column just inches from his head. Small pieces of debris were chipped off the structure, and some dust flew into Recker's eyes. He wiped them, and just as his vision was restored, he heard the sound of an engine revving. It was coming from his right, though he couldn't see the car yet. If it was Kaiser, he'd have to go right past him in order to leave. But Recker would have to be careful, because if he made himself visible, the shooter out there would likely be able to plug him.

Seconds later, the sound of more gunfire was heard, coming from the area Recker thought the shooter was. It was beyond a small group of cars, likely that of the others that worked there. Then a white sports car emerged from Recker's right. The windows were tinted, so he couldn't see inside, but he knew it had to be Kaiser. The car was speeding up in an effort to escape. It wouldn't be anyone else.

"Mike, you're good!" Haley yelled. The sound of gunfire was him taking out the shooter. Recker was now in the clear. "Take him!"

Recker stepped away from the column as the car continued in its path. He took aim at the vehicle and started firing his weapon. He took a couple shots at the tires, then put several rounds through the driver's side window. The car instantly spun out of control and drove erratically, and moments later plowed right into the side of another car. Recker and Haley immediately ran toward the vehicle.

"I'll get him," Recker said. "Keep an eye out."

Haley spun around, and while he kept moving with Recker, his back was turned to him. Haley's head was moving left to right, and back again, making sure there was nobody else with a gun pointed at them.

With Haley standing guard, once Recker got to the car, he tried pulling on the door. It was locked. He didn't have time to play with it. He took his gun in his left hand and forcefully smashed the window with it. Once the glass shattered, Recker quickly got into position, and aimed his gun at Kaiser, just in case the man decided to come up shooting.

Luckily, there was none of that. Kaiser's face was pressed against the airbag, which had deployed. He was still moving, though. Recker reached in, and grabbed the man by the collar, shifting him back against his seat.

"Eamon Kaiser, I presume?"

Kaiser slowly shook his head, his speech somewhat slurred. "I don't know who that is."

Recker laughed. "Yeah. I bet."

Kaiser appeared injured. He had a bullet wound in his left shoulder, and some cuts on his forehead and cheek, some of which may have been from the glass shattering. Recker reached inside and unlocked the door, opening it. He then grabbed Kaiser and pulled him out of the car, Kaiser's body hitting the ground.

"What do you want? What do you want with me?!"

Recker pulled him up to his feet. "You're about to find out."

"I don't think I can walk." Kaiser started faking a limp.

Recker laughed, not buying it for a second. "You're fine. Move."

"Do I know you guys?"

Recker and Haley each grabbed hold of one of Kaiser's arms, and escorted him back to the house.

Once inside, they stepped over the bodies again, and dragged him into the living room, shoving him down onto a couch.

"So what do you guys want? I mean, whatever, just ask. I can pay whatever." There was a look of fear in the man's eyes, one that wasn't common for him. He was used to instilling fear into other people. This was unusual for him. But he'd do anything he had to do to get out of it.

"Mac Webb, Logan Harris, and... what's that other guy's name?" Recker asked.

"Rory Zouch," Haley replied.

"I don't know why I keep forgetting that one. With a name like that, you'd think I'd remember."

Haley grinned. "Maybe old age creeping up on you."

"Might be." Recker turned his attention back to Kaiser. "Anyway, those are the names. We want them."

"What makes you think I can help?" Kaiser answered. "I don't know them."

Recker wasn't in the mood for games. He'd already played enough of them lately. And he didn't look amused. He leaned forward, and put his hand on Kaiser's wounded shoulder. "That looks kind of bad. You should probably get it looked at soon."

"Yeah, good idea. How 'bout letting me go so I can do that?"

Recker didn't respond. He simply pushed in on the

shoulder, making Kaiser scream in agony. Recker kept up the pressure for about five seconds.

"Sounds like that hurt," Recker said. "And that was only a few seconds. I wonder what the pain would feel like if we did that for a few minutes?"

Kaiser clutched at his shoulder as the pain slowly became less intense. He blew air through his mouth. "What do you guys want?"

"We already told you. Webb, Harris, Zouch. You know them."

"But I don't."

Recker instantly put his hand on Kaiser's shoulder again and pushed, a little harder than before. Kaiser let out another scream. Recker kept up the pressure for a few more seconds this time.

"How much longer you wanna do this?" Recker asked.

Kaiser didn't respond at first, letting the pain subside again. "Who are you guys, anyway?"

"We're ghosts. We're invisible. We don't exist. And if we choose, we can make it so you'll never be found again."

"What're you guys, government?"

"We ask the questions. And you've only got so much longer to answer them."

Kaiser scoffed, puffing his lips out. "I ain't talking to the likes of you. You guys can screw yourself."

Recker looked at Haley and smiled. "Guess he wants to do it the hard way."

"Looks like it," Haley replied.

Kaiser began looking concerned again. "What's the hard way?"

Recker pulled out his gun and pointed it at Kaiser's other shoulder. "This is the hard way. I start blowing holes in every other part of your body until you're in so much pain you'll wish you were dead. Only you won't be. And I can keep you alive, but in a lot of pain for a very long time."

Kaiser put his hands up in front of him, hoping to persuade him to do otherwise. "No, no, no. Please don't. No."

"Then tell us what we want to know."

"OK, if I do, what do I get out of it?"

Recker looked at his partner and laughed. "Listen to this guy. He thinks he can actually make demands or something. The only thing I can guarantee you'll get out of it is that I won't put more holes in you."

Kaiser took a few deep breaths, looking at both Recker and Haley. "You promise me you won't kill me? Or shoot me again?"

"If you're straight up and honest with us, you got my word. No more holes."

Kaiser sighed. "Man, you guys are the worst. You're worse than some criminals I know."

Recker looked unconcerned. "Do tell."

"You guys must work for the CIA or something. That's it, isn't it?"

Recker slowly pointed his gun at him again. "Webb. Harris. Zouch. That's all we want from you."

"You realize if this gets back to me, it'll ruin my reputation. You know that, right?"

Getting tired of his talking, Haley joined his partner in pointing his gun at their prisoner.

"The names," Recker said.

"Jeez, you guys, man. You must be fun at parties."

"Last time we ask."

"OK, OK. I know them."

"We already know that. We've seen your phone records."

"If you already know, then what do you want?"

"We want to know where to find him," Recker answered.

"If you're looking for a home address or something, I'm afraid I can't help you there. We don't conduct business that way."

"Exactly what is your business with them?"

"That's personal, man."

Recker moved his gun directly in front of the man's forehead. "This will be personal, too. And I'm not asking again."

"OK. OK. Just relax."

"We're looking for them, and you're gonna help us find them."

"OK, I only know about Webb. I know the others, but don't know where they are. Only Webb's here right now."

"We know that," Recker said.

"Like I said, I don't know where he's staying. He's not from around here, you know. We communicate through the phone, or messages, things like that. We don't meet in person."

"What is your business with him?"

"I'm a facilitator. I help bring parties together."

"I thought that's what he did?" Haley asked. "We already know what they're doing here. We know about the shipment."

"Oh. If you know about that, then what do you want?"

"What exactly are you facilitating?" Recker asked.

"Well these boys, Webb and them, have been here off and on for a while now, talking about some deal they had lined up. They apparently have the connections overseas, and they needed some help over here."

"Help with what?"

"Trying to find people who'd be interested in the kind of shipment they had. Help in figuring out where to bring it in, what to do with it after it came in, where to store it after it came in, things like that."

"And you get a cut, I take it?" Haley asked.

"Yeah, I get a little sumthin' sumthin'."

"So you know where the shipment is, then," Recker said. "We know it already came in."

"I mean, I know of some places it might have gone. I don't know exactly. I just gave them some ideas. What they did with it was up to them."

"OK. Well, we need you to get in touch with them."

"And say what?!"

"Something's gone wrong. You need to meet."

Kaiser started shaking his head. "No way, man, no way. He ain't gonna buy that. That's not how we operate. He'll think something's up right off the top."

"You make him believe it."

"I can't make lemonade with apples, man."

"Who's behind this shipment?" Haley asked. "Where's it coming from?"

"Couldn't tell you. Don't know. Don't care. That's not my business. My business is helping them get rid of it. All I know is it came from Europe. Where it was before that, like I said, don't know, don't care."

"Sounds like we're not getting very much for our bargain here," Recker said. "I might have to do something about that."

Kaiser immediately knew what he was referring to. "No, no, man, come on."

"We want your help. If you can't, or won't, give it to us, then we'll have to make alternate arrangements. And that means we won't need you anymore."

"Man, what assurance do I got that you won't kill me if I help you, anyway?"

Recker cleared his throat. "Well, I'm giving you my word I won't kill you. Maybe that means something to you, maybe not. The point is... if you tell us nothing, we're definitely gonna kill you. So you might as well tell us what you know and help us, and take the chance that we'll actually let you go afterward. Because the alternative to that is... death. Yours."

Kaiser sighed, knowing he had no other options but to trust the man. "Fine. Fine. What do you want me to do?"

"I want you to get in contact with Mac Webb for us. Tell him you want to meet."

Kaiser immediately started shaking his head. "No, no, won't work. Won't work."

"Why not?"

"Because that's not how it works. We do not just meet out of the blue. If I call and ask to meet somewhere, he'll know it's a trap. He's no dummy."

"Even if you say it's an emergency?"

Kaiser shrugged in a defiant manner. "What kind of emergency? What would be so important we'd have to meet right away? As you said, the shipment is already here. It's already been taken care of. He's already meeting with buyers. There's nothing more to say."

"What if you got word that someone's on to him?" Haley asked. "And you're trying to save him? Help him out."

Kaiser shook his head. "No. He's more on top of those things than I am. If someone's on his tail, like you two, he knows about it already. As a matter of fact, he'll probably assume you're behind me calling him about it. Does he already know of you two?"

"He does."

Split Scope

"See? Anything I do to try and get him out of his normal routine, he will assume it's a trap. Guaranteed."

"Do you know who's behind this shipment?" Recker asked.

"Told you, not my business. Webb knows. Where it's coming from, their business, where it's going, my business. That's how it works."

"And where is it going?"

"Hasn't been decided yet."

"Well you better come up with something good soon, 'cause you're not leaving here until you do. There's gotta be something that won't make him suspicious."

Kaiser slightly turned his head, as if he were thinking about it. A look came across his face, giving Recker and Haley the indication that something had crossed the man's mind.

"What is it?" Recker asked. "You thought of something?"

Kaiser raised one of his hands. "Uh, maybe. Maybe. I dunno."

"Might as well say it out loud."

"Well, the only thing I could say to him that wouldn't make him suspicious at the moment is that I possibly have a buyer in mind. That would require you meeting with him. I could say I have people who are interested, set up a meeting, then you take it from there."

Haley immediately put the brakes on that plan.

"We can't do that. Based on what happened outside that building when he tried to blow us up, we've gotta assume he had someone watching. That means he knows what we look like. If we show up to some meeting, he's gonna have us scanned long before we actually come face to face with him."

Recker nodded. He knew that was likely true.

"But time is also running short," Kaiser said. "Even for a deal. They want to have this wrapped up in the next day or two, I believe."

"What are they planning after that?" Haley asked.

"Who knows? As far as I know, they're setting up the deal, and as soon as an agreement is struck, they will be on their way."

"Will they be coming back?"

"Not to my knowledge. As you've astutely pointed out already, the merchandise is already here. Whoever wins will get further instructions when the time is right to release the rest of their winnings."

"Wait a minute," Recker said. "That's you, isn't it? That's your job. Whoever wins, in a couple of months, they get a call from you telling them where to pick up the rest of their stuff."

Kaiser grinned. "Guilty. But I don't know where the stuff is yet."

"You're telling me they're gonna trust you to know where it's at while they're gone, but they don't trust you to tell you where it's at right now?"

"Not at all. The way it works is they will call me

with a location on the morning of the second transaction, when the buyer's able to pick up the rest of their merchandise. I will lead them to that location and make sure everyone is satisfied and the transaction is complete. So no, they don't trust me either." Kaiser let out a laugh. "I guess they figure even I might have some evil plans in mind if I know where a fifty million stash of stuff is located, just sitting there for the taking for a couple months."

"Yeah, nice friends."

"So how are we gonna play this?" Haley asked.

Recker thought for a few moments. They had to get a meeting with Webb. If that was the only way, they'd have to somehow make it happen. It was just a question of who?

"I got someone," Recker said. "Someone we know. Someone we trust."

21

Even before they had Kaiser call Webb to tell him there was a new player in the game, Recker called Jones to tell him his plan. They didn't have time to waste. It was a two-hour drive from Philadelphia to Baltimore, and they weren't sure how long they could prolong this new meeting, assuming Webb would allow one, so Jones had to get there quickly. Recker and Haley were standing at the far edge of the room, away from Kaiser so he couldn't hear them talking.

"You sure about this?" Haley asked.

"David can do it," Recker answered.

"But, you didn't even tell him the plan. He doesn't even know he's the one going in yet."

Recker grinned. "Yeah. He'll be fine."

"What happens if he decides he won't do it?"

"He'll do it. He'll moan and complain for a few

minutes, but once he sees it's the only option, he'll do it. It'll be fine."

Haley raised his eyebrows. "Man, I'm sure glad you're so confident, 'cause I'm not so sure."

"Well we don't have time to argue about it, and if I tell him the plan now, and he procrastinates for a while, we might lose the advantage."

"I dunno. You might be the only one who thinks we have some kind of advantage right now."

"Positive thinking."

"Is that what it is?"

"That's what I'm going with at the moment."

Haley laughed. "Yeah. OK. Well, guess we might as well get this guy to play the rest of the part."

Recker and Haley walked across the room, back to the couch that Kaiser was still sitting on, holding his shoulder.

"Am I gonna be able to get medical attention for this at some point?" Kaiser asked.

"Yeah," Recker replied. "As soon as you do what we need you to do."

"You want me to call Webb and set something up?"

"We do."

"And what if he doesn't go for it?"

"You make him go for it. Because if he doesn't, that shoulder's going to be the least of your problems."

Kaiser sighed. "And they say the criminals are bad."

"You just don't like it when we play the same game that you do… only better."

"Fine, fine, whatever. Just give me a phone."

"Where's yours?" Haley asked.

"I dunno, I got a bunch of them." Kaiser pointed to the kitchen. "Just go in there. I got a whole drawer full. Just pick one."

Haley came back in a minute later, and handed a phone to Kaiser. Before he was able to call Webb, Recker had some last-minute instructions for him.

Recker pointed his finger at him. "Remember, you say anything to intentionally throw this deal off, you're as good as dead."

"I got it, I got it. I believe you. What exactly do you want me to do?"

"Set up a meeting. Tell him you got a guy named David Jones who wants to meet. Tell him he's new, but he's looking to ramp up his organization, and his power, quickly."

"Time frame?"

"Three, four, five hours. No earlier than three."

Kaiser looked dejected, but he had little choice in what he was about to do. "Got it."

"If you say anything…"

"I got it, I got it. You don't need to keep reminding me. At this point, I'm on your side. Because if Webb finds out I did this, I'm as good as dead. So what's best for me right now is for you guys to find him and take him out. Then I can play another day."

"Make the call," Recker said.

Kaiser dialed the number, then put the phone on

speaker, and held it out in front of him. Webb picked up after the third ring.

"I wasn't anticipating you calling again," Webb said.

"Yeah, well, I wasn't either," Kaiser replied. "But I got wind of something, wanted to throw it past you."

"What is it?"

"New player in the game. Guy named David Jones. Upstart, looking to make a name for himself. Wants to challenge some of the big dogs, if you know what I mean."

"Yeah? And?"

"Word is he might be willing to pay a steep price to get an advantage in the game. Something like what you got could give him a big head start."

"We're picking the winner tomorrow," Webb said.

"I know, I know. Just wanted to throw it out there, see what you thought. This guy might be willing to completely lap everyone else with an offer, though. He's got big pockets, and he wants to make them even bigger. Up to you, man, just thought I'd let you know. Might be worth your while."

"Is this guy on the level?"

"Completely. Already ran some checks on him. Could be a regular source for you and your supplier in the future if you come to terms. Like I said, just thought I'd run it by you. If it's too late, or you're not interested, no sweat to me. Just wanted to throw it out there."

Webb loudly sighed into the phone. "OK, maybe I can meet with this guy. It's gotta be today, though."

"Yeah, that's no problem. Already told him it probably had to be today."

"OK. Let's make it two hours from now."

"Oh, uh, I'm not sure that's gonna work." Kaiser looked up at Recker, who had three fingers up. "Uh, can you make it three? The guy's driving in here now, not sure he can get here in time. Think he's coming down from Philly or something."

"Fine. Three hours. No more."

"That should do it," Kaiser said. "If he can't make it by then, he can't make it. Where do you want him to go?"

"Are you seeing him once he gets there?"

"Uh, I dunno, wasn't planning on it. I mean, I guess I can if that's what you prefer."

"I'll text you an address in two and a half hours. You let me know if the guy's ready. If not, I'm moving on. If he is, I'll text you and tell him where to go."

"All right, man, sounds good."

They hung up, and Kaiser put the phone down next to him, which Haley promptly took away.

"How'd I do?" Kaiser asked.

Recker and Haley looked satisfied. "Nice," Recker said.

"Who's this Jones guy?"

"Nobody you need to worry about."

"Hey, I mean, not to keep bugging you guys or

anything, but can I get someone to fix my shoulder now? Please?"

Recker and Haley glanced at each other, neither really wanting to help, but figured they should since Kaiser seemed to be cooperating. Haley was the first to move, and got in closer to take a look at the man's shoulder.

"Ah, looks like it'll be OK," Haley said. "Bullet went straight through."

"And that's good?"

"Better than someone having to cut you open to get the bullet out."

As Haley worked on Kaiser's shoulder, Recker made a call to Lawson, letting her know what they had going on.

"Can you spare us some time?" Lawson asked. "I can get a team there."

"Can't," Recker said. "This was all we could get. I really would like to capture Webb, make him tell us what he knows."

"Well, that's how we'll try to play it, but I can't make any promises. David's going in there, and I'm not going to take a chance on his life just to get this guy in one piece. If it's one or the other, you know who I'll choose."

"Of course. That's not even a question. Are you sure there's no other way? Because if you don't mind me saying so, I think we both know how this meeting will likely go."

"Maybe. We'll see."

"And by the way, are you sure it's wise to let David go in there alone?" Lawson asked. "I mean, Webb is not some regular slob we're talking about here. I know David's not used to this type of thing, and if he's not on top of his game, Webb could kill him before he even knows what's going on."

"I've got provisions for that. And he's not going in alone."

"But I thought you said you couldn't chance you or Haley going in?"

"We're not," Recker answered. "He's gonna have someone else in there with him."

"Someone you trust?"

"Absolutely."

"Someone that can handle themselves if something goes bad?"

"Definitely."

"Someone that's not afraid if the odds are against them?"

"Odds don't scare him."

"Who are we talking about?"

Recker laughed. "As the CIA likes to say, that's on a need to know basis. And you don't need to know."

"Mike."

"Believe me, we've got this figured out. We'll try to take Webb, if possible. And if it's not, I'm sorry in advance."

"OK. Just let me know when it's done, OK?"

"Will do."

After getting off the phone with Lawson, Recker waited in the corner of the room until Haley was done patching up Kaiser's shoulder. Haley walked over to him.

"Nothing to do now but wait, I guess."

Recker nodded. "Yeah." He looked at the time. There was still a lot of time before Jones got there. "Nothing to do but wait."

22

Recker was looking out the window and saw Jones' car pull up in front of the house. He walked out to meet Jones as he got out of his car. Jones' eyes instantly saw a body.

"Do you not worry in the least about the police showing up?"

Recker shrugged. "Lawson said she could keep the area clean for a few more hours. She's got some pull."

"Nice to have friends in high places." They walked inside. "So what's this about?"

Recker let out a nervous laughter. He then began explaining everything. He was just about finished when Haley came over to them. When Recker finally did finish, Jones stood there, looking paralyzed. He stared at Recker. Recker and Haley looked at each other.

"Not quite the reaction I anticipated," Recker said.

Haley agreed. "Maybe he's in shock."

"David?"

Jones seemed to snap free of his stare. "So what you are saying is you want me to meet with this killer? This ex-MI6 agent?"

"Uh, yeah, that's about the size of it."

"And you have no qualms about this?"

"Oh, I have plenty. I just think you can do it."

"And why would you think that? Your expertise is in the field, not mine. Mine's behind a desk."

"We all have to step outside our comfort zones every now and then," Recker said.

"This isn't stepping, this is leaping off a cliff into the ocean. I'm not sure I can pull this off on my own."

"You won't be on your own."

"You said you and Chris would be on the outside."

"We will."

"Then who else is there?"

Recker was just about to answer when he heard another car pulling up. "Looks like we're about to find out."

They all went over to a window and looked out, seeing Jimmy Malloy walking toward the house.

Jones took a step back and turned toward his partner. "Please tell me you're not serious."

"Why not? You'll be as safe with him as you are with us."

Malloy then walked through the door, greeting everyone as he saw them. "We ready to do this yet?"

"Still waiting for a call," Recker replied. "Should be in a few minutes."

Malloy playfully smacked Jones on the arm. "Bet you never thought I'd be your bodyguard, huh?"

Jones' eyes opened wide. "Uh, no, no, I didn't."

"You sure you're up for this?" Recker asked.

"Yeah, let's do it," Malloy answered. "Let's take out these bums."

"You didn't even ask me if I'm up for it," Jones said. "I mean, do I get a choice?"

"Sure," Recker said. "But if you don't, then we have no other option at the moment. And that means Webb's probably getting away. And the rest of them too, most likely."

"So it all rests on me."

"You got it."

"Don't worry, David," Malloy said. "I got you. Nothing to worry about."

"That somehow doesn't make me feel better."

"These guys ain't no big deal. If he's like the last one I met, nothing to it. Piece of cake."

"Well now I just feel wonderful about it."

"If you're uneasy about it, you don't have to," Recker said.

"No, no, as you said, we must all do our part and step out of our comfort zones sometimes. I'll do what has to be done."

While they waited for Webb to text Kaiser, the team started preparing themselves for what was about to go down. It was mostly about getting Jones prepared, making sure he said the right things. They were counting on Malloy to help him out if need be. Wherever this meeting was to take place, Recker and Haley were going to be outside, as close as they could be.

The plan was actually for nothing to happen inside. They hoped that Jones could learn something useful, either about the other men, or about the shipment, and then leave. Then once Webb left, Recker and Haley would have him in their sights. Then they could either take him out, or convince him to surrender, whichever was more likely, though they already assumed which option that would be.

Once it was thirty minutes to the meeting time, a text message came in on Kaiser's phone. Haley was the first to look at it.

"Here's the address." Haley read it and looked at Kaiser. "You know it?"

Kaiser nodded. "Yeah, I know it."

"What and where is it?"

"It's about twenty... twenty-five minutes away."

"Means we're not gonna be able to get there ahead of time," Recker said.

"Pretty sure it's a vacant retail store, went out of business a few years ago."

"And anybody goes in to use it?"

Kaiser grinned. "People have their ways, you know?"

"Wait, there's more," Haley said, reading the message. He looked at Kaiser. "He wants you to go too."

"What?! No, that's not part of the deal."

Haley tossed the phone over to him. "Read it yourself."

"What? No! I can't go."

"Why not?"

"What if there's more shooting? What if he thinks I'm setting him up?"

"Then I guess you'll be the first to go."

"No, I can't go."

"You either take your chances there, or you die here," Recker said. "Your choice."

"Awe, man, this sucks."

"Let's go."

"Wait. What's he gonna say when he sees my shoulder?"

"Nothing. Go get a new shirt. Cover it up."

Haley went up to Kaiser's room and got him a new shirt. Once everyone was ready, they left together. They took their separate cars to leave, figuring there was no need to come back there again. Though Jones would park his car in a nearby lot to get in Malloy's car, along with Kaiser, since it wouldn't look right if they arrived at the meeting spot separately. As they traveled to the meeting spot, Recker and Haley were right behind Malloy's car.

They arrived at the spot in just under twenty-five minutes. Malloy pulled up near the building, which already had several other cars there. Recker and Haley immediately tried finding another spot nearby. There were other buildings in the area on both sides of it. They had to assume Webb had some sort of exit strategy in mind, just in case this meeting wasn't what he thought it was. That meant Recker and Haley splitting up.

Recker went to the building across the street from it, looking to head up to the roof in order to give himself a clear shot of the entrance. Haley would go around the building to the back of it, which would take more time, but he'd be able to get there before Webb came out.

Malloy stepped out of the car, then went to the back door and opened it for Jones and Kaiser. As the three of them stood there for a moment, Malloy looked around.

"Keep your eyes open," Malloy said.

"And what if things start to get hairy?" Jones asked.

"Just leave everything to me. I'll let you know if things are about to get rough."

"How?"

"I'll tell you your shoe's untied. If I say that... hit the dirt."

"What about me?" Kaiser asked.

"Same thing. Hit the ground. Hard."

"I hate this."

Malloy then saw the boarded-up door opening. A man appeared. Tough-looking guy in his late twenties.

He folded his arms and stood there, apparently waiting for Jones and company to get there.

"This is it," Malloy said.

Jones took a deep breath. "I don't know why I'm so nervous for this."

"Relax. I'll get you out of here in no time. Trust me."

They walked around the car and toward the opened door where the man was standing. He stepped aside as the group walked in. There was another man standing there, ready to greet them.

"Mr. Jones?"

Jones nodded. "That's me. Are you Mr. Webb?"

The middle-aged man shook his head, then stuck his right arm out. "This way."

The man started walking to his right, with Jones and company following him. They went through a door, then down a hallway, which had doors on both sides. It appeared this was the office area of whatever business that used to occupy the space. They eventually stopped as they came to the last door on the left. The man opened it. It looked like it might have been a manager's office, since there was still a desk in the room.

Sitting behind the desk was Mac Webb. The room was lined with more of his associates, as well. There were four guys standing to Webb's left, leaning up against the wall. There were four others to his right, also leaning up against the wall.

"Mr. Jones?" Webb asked, standing up to greet them. Jones walked over to him and shook hands. "Have a seat." Webb pointed to a metal chair in front of his desk.

"Thank you."

"I understand you're looking to do a little business."

"That's correct. I've already been informed by Mr. Kaiser as to the particulars of the situation."

Webb's eyes briefly darted over to Kaiser, who looked a little uncomfortable being there. Webb's eyes returned to Jones. "And the cost is something that you're willing to surrender?"

"It is. I understand fifty million will get the job done?"

"Well, I mean, around there. It will be a closed bidding process. You've got one chance. One bid. Whoever's the highest. Could be fifty. Could be a lot more. I simply don't know yet."

"I see. And is there something I could do to give myself an edge in that regard?"

"Well, you could go well over the expected winning bid to give yourself the best chance."

"Or, perhaps an extra fee to see what the winning bid is with a chance to match?"

Webb smiled. "Mr. Jones, that would be unethical of the process here, wouldn't it?"

"I'm sorry. I thought this was a business dealing. Not an ethical one."

"And is there something you have in mind?"

"Oh, I don't know, maybe an extra million dollars, just for having the right to see that winning bid, and put in something higher. And maybe an extra fee on top of whatever the winning bid is? Say... ten million more?"

Webb leaned back in his chair. For someone who seemed to be getting offered a good deal, he didn't appear to be that thrilled about it. He looked down at his hands, which he had clasped together.

"What do you say, Eamon?" Webb asked.

"Me?"

"You. Can you vouch for him? Think he's good for the extra money?"

Kaiser looked at Jones, then Malloy, then back at Webb. He was getting more nervous by the second. "Uh, yeah, yeah, I think so. Yeah. He's good for it."

Malloy continued to stand there, only barely listening to the conversation between Webb, Jones, and Kaiser. They kept talking, but Malloy's eyes were bouncing all over the place. He looked at Webb, then his guards, and continued the pattern. He could see it in Webb's voice, his mannerisms, that he didn't believe a word that Jones was saying. Or Kaiser, for that matter.

This was a trap. There was no doubt in Malloy's mind. Webb didn't believe for a second that this was a regular business deal. He knew that this was a setup, just like the last person that tried to contact him for a deal. For all Webb knew, it was the same people behind it.

As the trio continued talking, Malloy started running through the scenarios in his mind. It was basically nine against one, not that he was so much concerned with the odds. But he figured at some point, Webb was going to get tired of this charade, and order his men to fire. Malloy was going to have to make sure that he beat them to the punch. Right now, the guards were still standing somewhat aloof, some of their hands behind their backs, some by their sides. But none of them appeared to be in a fighting pose yet.

"Do you happen to have a sample of the merchandise that I could inspect?" Jones asked.

"Un, no, I don't," Webb replied. "Sorry."

"Oh. Well, how can I be sure that it's of the highest quality?"

"I guess you can't."

Malloy figured now was as good a time as any. The conversation seemed like it was about to wrap up. He needed to act fast. He cleared his throat.

"Uh, boss, looks like your shoe's untied."

Jones' eyes immediately started rolling around. He dropped to the ground, as did Kaiser, just as Malloy removed two pistols, one in each hand. Malloy started taking aim at the guards, starting with the ones at the ends and making his way inward. One by one, the guards fell like dominoes. It wasn't until the last two guards remaining that Malloy got a response. The guards were able to pull their guns, but were unable to mount any kind of defense. And only one of them was even able to fire back, though the bullet missed Malloy by a wide margin.

Everything went down in a matter of seconds. As his guards started to fall, Webb reached into the drawer of his desk to pull out a pistol. He stood up, just as the last of his guards were taken out. He didn't have the advantage. By now, Malloy had both guns pointed at him, while Webb still had his gun down by his side. If Webb attempted to fire, he wouldn't be successful. He knew it. Now, he just had to do what he could to stay alive.

"What do you guys want?" Webb asked.

Jones and Kaiser now stood up.

"We would like the locations of your partners, for one," Jones said.

"Won't happen."

"And we would like to know where that shipment is."

"Won't happen, either," Webb said.

"Then this conversation's pointless," Malloy said, fully ready to fire two more shots to end the conflict.

"There's gotta be something else."

"How about the name of your supplier?" Jones asked.

"Can't tell you that either."

"Exactly what can you tell us?"

Webb really wasn't about to tell them anything of

value. But those guards in the room weren't the only men he had there. He was just waiting for the rest to appear.

Seconds later, the door burst open. Two more of Webb's men came charging in. As soon as they did, Webb finally brought his gun up in front of him. He was hoping to use the diversion in order to kill the men in front of him, starting with Malloy, since he seemed to be the most dangerous.

His plan didn't work, though. Malloy also knew who the most dangerous man in the room was, other than himself. As soon as the door broke open, Malloy fired two rounds, both of which hit Webb in the middle of his chest. As he fell to the floor, Malloy dove to the floor himself, then quickly found his new targets.

Jones and Kaiser also hit the ground, trying to get out of harm's way. As the two men rushed into the room, bullets from Malloy's gun found each of them. Seconds later, they also dropped to the ground. Kaiser cried out in pain, getting hit in the crossfire of one of the encounters.

"You gotta be kidding me!" Kaiser yelled. "Not again! Twice in one day!"

As Malloy left the room to make sure there was nobody else to shoot at, Jones went over to Kaiser to check his condition.

"Are you all right?"

"No!" Kaiser shouted. "I've been shot! Again!"

Jones looked at the man's body and saw traces of blood seeping through his shirt. "Here, let me take a look." Jones lifted Kaiser's shirt up and took a closer look at the man's condition. "Looks like it's just a scratch."

"A scratch?! Just a scratch?! Are you kidding me?! Feels like I'm on fire here!"

Jones let out a grin. He was used to dealing with men like Recker and Haley, who often downplayed their injuries, or failed to acknowledge they even had any. He'd forgotten that this was probably the way most people dealt with it.

"It appears like it just grazed your side. You should be fine."

"Oh, man, why me? What did I ever do?"

Seconds later, Malloy came back into the room. "OK. Looks like we're clear." Jones got up, though Kaiser remained on the floor. Malloy looked down at him. "Yo, dude, we gotta go!"

"Just let me lay here."

"Fine, when the police come, they can say you're responsible for everything."

Kaiser's eyes widened. He didn't like the sound of that proposition. He instantly got up to his feet, though he still had his hand on his side. "Hey, whaddya know? Feeling better already."

"Yeah, thought you might. Let's get out of here."

They started to leave the room, then Jones stopped, looking back in the direction of the desk. "Wait for me." Jones went back into the room, straight for Webb's body. Jones dug into the man's pockets, hoping to find something of interest. And he found it in Webb's left front pocket. Jones held Webb's phone up, looking satisfied. He then darted out of the room, quickly catching up with Malloy and Kaiser.

Minutes later, the three of them were out of the building. Jones got on his phone and called Recker, not sure exactly where he was.

"How'd it go in there?" Recker asked.

"It's over. At least this part of it. Webb's dead."

"Happen to get anything out of him."

"No, he was very tight-lipped about everything."

"Figures. Back to the drawing board, I guess."

Jones held Webb's phone and looked at it. "Maybe not. We might have something after all."

23

The team traveled back to Philadelphia, with Haley driving Jones' car, so Jones could work in the back seat as they drove. They knew they had no time to waste on this, as it wouldn't be long until the remaining two ex-MI6 agents knew that Webb was now gone, too. When they arrived in the parking lot, Jones flew out of the car to get back to the office.

Haley stood there for a moment, waiting for his partner to arrive, which he did just a couple of minutes later. After Recker got out of his car, they walked together back to the office.

"You think we did the right thing letting Kaiser go?"

"We made a deal with him," Recker replied. "Besides, I gave Lawson everything we had on him. I doubt he'll be living free too much longer, anyway."

"What if he warns the others?"

Recker shook his head. "After everything that went

down, that guy's getting as far away from this as he can. He knows the walls are closing in."

By the time Recker and Haley actually stepped foot in the office, Jones was furiously working between two computers, looking like he'd been like that all day. Recker and Haley went over to him, standing behind him to see what was on the monitors.

"You look like you've got something," Recker said. "But I can't be sure what."

Jones stopped typing and moved his chair to the side so he could look at both of them directly. He had a grin on his face. "I've got them."

"You know where they are?"

Jones put a finger in the air. "They're both on the move right now."

"Well then how do you know where they are?"

"Webb talked to each of them within the last twenty-four hours. Phone calls and texts. I was able to use that to locate their exact positions by bouncing the signals off of cell phone towers, IP addresses, et cetera, et cetera. So now, I've got a line on the phones they were using to contact Webb."

"So you know where these guys are going?"

"I have an idea," Jones answered. He went back to a computer and pulled up a map. "Here." He pointed to the screen. "I've put up two red dots, signaling the positions of Harris and Zouch. They're both moving down."

"OK?" Haley said, still not seeing the big picture. "How's that tell us where they're going?"

"Right now, my theory is that they're heading here."

Recker and Haley both looked at him with a surprised look on their face. "Here?" Recker asked. "As in Philadelphia?"

"Yes."

"What makes you say that?"

"Logical deduction."

"What's logical about it?"

"I don't know why we didn't see it before." Jones turned to the map again. "Look at this. Baltimore, Newark, New York, Boston. What major city is between all of them?"

"Philadelphia."

"And the two remaining members are moving down toward us. If we make the logical deduction that the shipment already came in, and that it's not in any of the cities that the men flew into, what's the next deduction?"

"But if they really wanted to be cute, that shipment could've gone into Delaware, Maryland, Virginia, and right on down the coast."

"It's my theory that they chose those cities initially, because they were all central to the place the shipment was really coming to. And it makes more sense that the shipment would come into a more dense area so it could blend in."

"They are moving in our direction," Haley said.

"Yeah, but is that because we're in the way of where they're really going?" Recker asked.

"I think not," Jones replied. "But anyway, let's not lose sight of the fact that wherever that shipment came in, it's probably not still there. It's already been established that it's been taken to another location. The problem is identifying that other location it's been transferred to."

Recker nodded, looking at the dots on the screen move. "So all we have to do is follow these guys and hope they lead us to it."

"I believe that would be the plan."

"How far away is Zouch from Harris?"

"Harris looks to be about an hour ahead of him," Jones said. "He left about forty-five minutes ago. Depending on traffic, if this is where he's headed, we have about an hour before he gets here."

"Zouch left before Harris?"

"Yes, he left several hours ago. Probably because Boston's further away, and I'm guessing they wanted to get here around the same time. But right now, I put him about an hour behind Harris."

"That means we'll have a little bit of time. Whenever Harris stops, we'll have to locate him quickly, then be ready for Zouch."

"Or just wait for both of them to meet up."

"Assuming they will. There's no guarantee they're going to do that. Especially once they find out about Webb."

"Puts us in a little bit of a jam, doesn't it?" Haley asked.

"How's that?" Recker said.

"Doesn't Lawson and the CIA want these guys alive? That way they can track down the source of this?"

Recker looked back at the screen. "I don't see how we're gonna accomplish that."

"By capturing them instead of killing them?" Jones said.

"Saying it's one thing. Doing it's another. Guys like this know what happens when you're caught. Especially now that they're ex-MI6, which means there's nobody coming for you. Nobody's coming to rescue you, and nobody's coming to exchange something for your release. You're on your own. It's not the same as doing a government sanctioned mission. Well, in some cases it is, but sometimes, you can hope someone's coming. These guys don't have that."

"Well, if they value their life, then?"

Recker shook his head. "Look at Corbyn and Webb. These guys would rather go down with the ship than surrender. They know what awaits them in a CIA prison. Believe me, they want no part of that."

"Unless they can be turned."

"David, you're talking out your ass right now. Nobody could trust these guys on an assignment. And Lawson prefers them dead, anyway. They just want to know the source of the shipment first before they get killed."

"I guess you're right, but what do we do, then?"

"If we can take one alive, we will. If we can find out who's behind the shipment, we will."

"And if we can't?" Haley asked.

"Then we do what we were brought in here to do in the first place," Recker replied. "We take them out. That's what we were initially asked to do."

"Missions change, though."

"I know. But finding who's behind this isn't really our mission."

Jones looked at his friend curiously. "It isn't? I thought our mission was to help and protect people, wherever that may lead. Doesn't finding the people responsible for bringing in fifty million dollars worth of heroin qualify?"

Recker sighed. "I hate it when you talk sense."

"Just want to understand where we're at in the ballgame."

"Or we could just turn everything over to Lawson and the CIA and let them handle it from here," Haley said. "They can follow them now."

Recker looked at Jones. "Is there a way they can see your computer so they can follow these guys on their end?"

"Sure there is. But if you think I'm going to let them share my computer and dig into my stuff in the background, you've got another thing coming."

"I've got an idea. You tell me how they can fixate on Zouch, so they can zoom in on him, and we'll take Harris ourselves."

"Now that is doable."

Their conversation was interrupted when Webb's phone started ringing. Jones picked it up and looked at the number. A worried look came over his face.

"It's Harris. What do we do?"

"We obviously can't answer it," Recker replied.

"If Webb doesn't pick up, what if that spooks him?"

Recker shrugged. "We'll just have to figure something out."

After the phone stopped ringing, Recker grabbed the phone. He immediately went to Harris' phone number and started typing a message. He was just playing it by ear. He figured if they waited too long, that would make Harris more suspicious than if they texted back right away.

"Hey, missed your call. I think I got someone on my tail here. Trying to lose them."

Harris texted back almost immediately. *"Who?"*

"Not sure. Trying not to lead them to you."

"Did you leave yet?"

"Yes, but I'm still in Maryland. Want me to keep coming?"

"No. Ditch whoever's behind you. I'll take care of the transaction. Get yourself on a plane and get out of here."

"Will do."

Recker put the phone down and looked at his partners. "Sure sounds to me like the deal's happening now."

"Then why would Webb have agreed to meet with me when he did?" Jones asked. "Wouldn't it have been too late in the game?"

"I think he knew it was a trap and was hoping to kill you."

"Oh. So what now?"

"We proceed as scheduled. I'll call Lawson. Just tell me how they can get a line on Zouch."

"I'll print everything out. Then you can just take a picture of it and send it to her. They should be able to pick it up from there."

"OK."

"But speaking of traps, if Webb knew I was a trap, then perhaps Harris knows you are too. Just because he said the right things, doesn't mean he believes that was Webb talking. People have a certain way of texting. And if his is usually different, he already knows that wasn't him."

Recker nodded. "I know. We'll just have to hope we're OK."

"And if we're not?"

"We'll cross that bridge when we come to it."

24

Wanting to get to Harris' position as quickly as possible, even though they didn't know where that would end up being yet, Recker and Haley left the office to meet him. They started driving in Harris' direction, and instructed Jones to let him know if he stopped somewhere. Even if being out on the road already saved them ten or twenty minutes, that could have been valuable time.

Recker and Haley were waiting just off one of the I-95 entrance ramps. As soon as Harris got near them, they could jump on the highway and follow him. If Harris got off the highway before reaching them, they could still get to him fairly quickly. It gave them plenty of time to think.

"Where do you think this is going?" Haley asked.

"I don't know. Could be anything, I suppose."

"The way I'm reading it, Harris isn't on to us yet."

"How you figure?"

"If he thought we were, would he still be coming in this direction? Wouldn't he go the opposite way? Or wouldn't he try to book the next flight out?"

"Might figure we're watching the planes."

"Maybe. Still wouldn't explain why he's coming this way."

Recker nodded. "Could be."

"And he can't know we're tracking his phone. Otherwise he'd ditch that thing."

They stayed in that position for a little while until they finally got word from Jones that Harris was approaching.

"He's getting off 95," Jones said.

Recker was surprised that Harris was getting off already. It was sooner than they expected. "What? Where?"

"Bensalem exit."

It turned out to be one of the best-case scenarios for them. They were sitting off the Woodhaven exit, which was just a few minutes away, so they didn't have to radically change course. With Haley behind the wheel, they immediately put the car in drive. Recker stayed on the phone with Jones so they could be informed about where Harris was going next.

"Where's he going?" Recker asked.

"He's on Street Road now, heading toward State," Jones replied.

Recker had an idea of where Harris might be going.

"There are some warehouses on State Road, might be heading there."

"Check that. He turned left onto Dunksferry."

"We're headed there."

A few seconds later, Jones updated the position. "Now he turned left onto Marshall Lane."

"Gotta be those warehouses over there," Haley said. "I know there's a few empty ones."

"He's now turned right onto Winks," Jones reported.

"We're about five minutes out," Recker said. "Keep us updated."

Recker and Haley were on State Road, going as fast as they could, and well over the speed limit. After a few minutes had passed, Recker wanted to know Harris' status.

"How's it looking?"

"It appears that he has stopped," Jones said.

"Good. Where?"

"He's still on Winks."

"We should be there in a minute or two, coming up from State."

"He hasn't moved. I've got your position on the same map. You're about to overlap."

"We're on State now," Recker said.

"Look to your left. You should be on him soon." They continued driving. "Stop. You're on top of him."

"There's an entrance to a warehouse. There's a gate across, though."

"That's where he is."

"All right. We'll have to go the rest of the way on foot."

Haley parked along the side of the road, a little further down, where there was some grass and trees. They got out of the car, pulled out a bag from the trunk, and went back to the warehouse entrance. Once there, they could see the iron fence go around the property.

"Looks like we're cutting our way in," Recker said.

Haley put the bag down and pulled out a pair of clippers. A minute later, they had a nice-sized hole to climb through. Once on the inside, they took a quick look around.

"Look out for cameras," Recker said. "Or he could see us long before we get there."

Haley pointed to the warehouse. "I see his car there, on the side of the building."

"Looks like he might be alone so far."

"If he's meeting someone, we should probably work fast. Otherwise we might have a lot more company than we want."

The problem for them was there was a lot of open space between where they were and the building. If someone was watching, there was a good chance one of them would get picked off. Maybe even both. There was absolutely nothing to duck behind for cover. But they were there now. It was a chance they'd have to take. Otherwise, they could go back to the car, and try to pick Harris up again when he left. But there was no guarantee they'd find a better spot than they had now. In fact, it could always be worse. And if there was one thing that Recker and Haley had learned over the years... things could always be worse.

Oftentimes, in a situation like this, Recker and Haley wouldn't move together. They'd stagger their releases, so they both wouldn't be caught in a barrage of gunfire at the same time. But in this case, they thought it would be better to move together. Moving separately, they thought they'd be easier to pick off.

Moments later, with guns in hand, they ran toward the building. They veered off to the left, trying to stay out of sight and range from the front window. About thirty seconds later, they made it. They clung to the side of the warehouse as they caught their breath.

Recker peeked around the edge of the building to the front, trying to figure out the best way to get in. There was no entrance on the side of the building they were on.

"You head around back," Recker said. "Look for the back door. I'll take the front."

"You want me to wait for anything?"

"No. As soon as you find it, you get inside as quick as you can. If it spooks him before I get in the front, I can still grab him."

Haley immediately took off, looking for the back door. Recker moved around the corner of the building, ducking his head under the windows in the front.

Once he reached the other front corner, he turned, seeing Harris' car sitting on the side.

Recker checked out the car first, making sure that Harris wasn't still in there. Once he cleared it, he turned and focused on the building. There was a door there, half glass. He turned the handle, but it was locked. He took a quick peek inside, but couldn't see much. It was just a small entrance to a small reception area, though there were no chairs or desks.

With no other way to approach it, Recker smashed the glass part of the door with his weapon. Once that broke, he reached inside and unlocked the door. He opened it and carefully looked inside, making sure he wasn't walking into a parade of bullets. With it looking clear, he went in.

Recker tapped his ear comm. "Chris, you in yet?"

"Just got in now."

"Me too. Keep a lookout."

Recker kept walking down a short hallway, which then led into the larger warehouse. He saw a large amount of boxes, and pallets, though they were all under sheets so he couldn't see what it was exactly. Seconds later, he noticed movement coming from the back of the room. He raised his gun in front of him, ready to fire. He then saw the outline of Haley's body come into view.

Recker and Haley looked at each other, both of them putting their hands up. Recker then spun around, looking up, looking toward the boxes and crates, wondering if Harris was hiding somewhere. He had to be. There weren't exactly a lot of other places he could have gone. By now, Haley had walked to the center of the room where his partner was.

"Where could he go?" Haley asked.

"I don't know. He's gotta be here somewhere."

Then another voice was heard. "Where, indeed?" Harris had now emerged from the same hallway that Recker had come through. With a grin on his face, Harris stretched his arms out wide. "Well, looks like you have found me. Here I am. Are you satisfied?"

"Just keep your hands where we can see them," Recker said.

"Well I guess that works for me. But what about them?" Harris looked to his left. Instantly, several more men entered the room, all holding a weapon, standing on each side of Harris.

Recker looked at the four men on each side of Harris. "Looks like you're still outnumbered."

Harris laughed. "I do like a confident opponent."

"Put your guns down, and I promise you we won't kill you."

Harris continued laughing. "Before I kill you, who are you working for that you've stuck your nose into things?"

"Not important."

"Oh, I think it is. Are you the ones that killed Corbyn?"

"Nope. Wasn't us."

"And what about Webb? Is he dead too?"

"Afraid so. That wasn't us either."

"For people who aren't behind anything, you sure got a funny way of popping up here. What do you want?"

"Who's behind the shipment?"

"Can't tell you."

"You mean won't."

Harris shrugged. "Whatever. Amounts to the same thing, I suppose. Any last words?"

"Yeah. Just this."

Recker and Haley immediately opened fire, hitting several of the men next to Harris. Luckily, the situation inside was better than it was outside. There were quite a bit of objects to get behind. And they needed it. The bullets were flying in every direction, with nobody letting up.

Recker and Haley had gotten the upper hand by surprising their opponents by firing first. Four of the men were killed right off the bat. Now there were only five left, which was much more manageable for the pair. The lobbying of gunfire back and forth went on for several more minutes, with neither side appearing to get the upper hand. Nobody else went down, and nobody moved in closer. It seemed like they were at a standstill.

"Hold your fire!" Harris yelled. "Hold your fire!"

"You want something?" Recker asked.

"Yeah. How about a truce?"

"I'm listening to your terms."

"Here are my terms. I'll let you two leave right now, and nobody else has to get hurt. I won't kill you. We'll just agree that you've lost this one."

"You think I was born yesterday? You just want to get us into a more favorable spot so you can kill us."

"No, that's not it. I'm a man of my word. If I say you can leave, you can bank on it as truth."

"Oh yeah?" Recker said. "Your friends at MI6 might not feel the same way. Double agents don't usually get that kind of respect."

"Oh, come on, that double agent thing is a bunch of malarkey. No proof."

"Secret government agencies don't need proof. Just suspicion. And sometimes that's more than enough."

"You sound like someone who's been through it."

"Maybe I have."

"Well then you should know that sometimes the truth isn't what's written down."

"What about the CIA agent you killed?" Recker asked.

There was a slight pause by Harris. "Wait, is that what this is about? Retaliation? Revenge? All because of one agent?"

"Isn't that enough?"

"Please, man, I mean, sometimes people get caught in the crossfire, you know? Anybody that was unlucky enough to go down, it wasn't intentional. Sometimes, that's just how it goes."

Recker took a peek around the boxes he was behind, and saw that none of their opponents were showing themselves. They were either taking a break, or reloading. Either way, it was an advantage for Recker and Haley. Recker quickly looked back at his partner and gave him some hand signals.

They both stood up, resting their weapons on top of their respective boxes to steady themselves, and waited for the first sign of movement from Harris' crew. Seconds later, two of the men raised their heads up. Recker and Haley fired simultaneously, hitting both men in the forehead, each of them instantly going down.

"Looks like you're down to three," Recker said. "And now you've got another problem."

"And what's that?"

"As soon as you show yourselves, we're blowing your heads off. And you can't escape, because I've got a clear line of sight to the door."

"Never get overconfident, mate. No matter how the odds look in your favor."

One of the men suddenly made a dash for the door, but Recker was able to cut him down before he even got halfway there.

"Looks like we're even now," Harris said.

"Nope. Now we've got you outnumbered."

Harris laughed. "I love the way you think, man. You sure you wouldn't like to come on my side. You can make a lot of money."

"Already make a lot of money."

"So what interests you? I'm sure we can agree to some kind of a deal."

"I doubt it."

The other remaining man, besides Harris, broke for the hallway, but was quickly gunned down by Haley.

"Doesn't seem like you have many options left," Recker said.

"Maybe to you," Harris replied.

"You can give yourself up, though."

Harris laughed. "What for? So I can be sent to some secret prison nobody knows about? So I can be tortured and questioned every day for the rest of my life? So they can kill me when I don't have any usefulness to them anymore? No thanks. That's no way to live."

"But at least it's living."

"Only cowards are afraid to die. And I'm no coward."

Harris stood up straight and started firing wildly, alternating in Recker and Haley's direction. It only lasted a few seconds, though. Once Recker ducked after the first round, while Harris was firing at Haley, Recker drilled Harris with four successive rounds. Harris fell to the ground, and Recker and Haley ran over to him. Any hopes of getting anything out of him was gone. Because Harris was too.

"Pretty much went down like you thought," Haley said.

"Yeah. Too bad."

"For who?"

"I dunno. For whoever wants information about that shipment."

Haley turned around. "Speaking of, let's take a look here."

They started taking the sheets off of everything, and took a peek in some of the boxes and crates. They got a little more than they bargained for. Not only did they find the heroin, but they found other drugs, as well. They also found several crates full of weapons.

"Either we didn't get the full story about what was being delivered, or they've been doing this longer than we think," Haley said.

"I'd opt for the latter. I mean, we know that Webb's been here other times, based on meeting Johnson. Wouldn't surprise me if this has been going on for a while."

"Doesn't look like we're gonna find out who's behind this."

"I dunno," Recker said. "Maybe they can grab Zouch, make him talk."

"Not so sure about that."

"Me neither. Either way, I think our job's done."

"Might as well call Lawson and let her know."

Recker nodded and pulled out his phone. Lawson

picked up after a few rings. Recker could already hear a bunch of voices in the background.

"You busy?"

"Oh, you know, just taking care of things," Lawson replied.

"Us too."

"How'd you make out with Harris?"

"He's dead."

"That's too bad."

"But, we did find that shipment."

"Really?"

"Yeah, we're standing next to it right now," Recker answered. "And that's not all. There's a lot more than that here. We're probably talking a few million more in other drugs, not to mention weapons. Might be looking at close to a hundred million dollars here."

"Wow. I'll get people there right away."

"Good. You don't need us to stick around and wait for them, do you?"

"I wasn't counting on it, and I wasn't thinking that you would, would you?"

"No."

"I thought not."

"We'll keep an eye on the place from a distance, though, at least until you get people here. Just so nobody shows up unexpectedly and cleans the place out."

"I'd appreciate that."

"How's Zouch? Still got an eye on him?"

"No, we actually just put him in handcuffs about ten minutes ago."

"Really? Didn't try to shoot his way out?" Recker asked.

"He wasn't given the chance. We sent him a message that looked like it came from Harris' phone. He pulled over in the spot we wanted and we took him. He got roughed up a little, so we'll see how it goes."

"Maybe you'll get the answers you were looking for."

"I don't know. Maybe. I'm sure we can persuade him somehow to talk. I hope, anyway."

"I guess that's it for us, then," Recker said. "Chalk another one up in the win column."

"Yeah. Hey, thanks. I know you didn't have to do this. And none of it would've been possible without you. You guys are what did this. I really do appreciate your work on it."

"Don't worry about it. We'll put your bill in the mail."

ABOUT THE AUTHOR

Mike Ryan is a USA Today Bestselling Author, and lives in Pennsylvania with his wife, and four children. He's the author of numerous bestselling books. Visit his website at www.mikeryanbooks.com to find out more about his books, and sign up for his newsletter. You can also interact with Mike via Facebook, and Instagram.

- facebook.com/mikeryanauthor
- instagram.com/mikeryanauthor

ALSO BY MIKE RYAN

Continue reading The Silencer Series with the next book, Firing Line.

The Extractor Series

The Eliminator Series

The Brandon Hall Series

The Cain Series

The Ghost Series

The Cari Porter Series

The Last Job

A Dangerous Man

The Crew

Printed in Great Britain
by Amazon